"Tyce."

Sage called his name again. He lifted his head and looked at her with those intensely dark, pain-filled eyes.

"Take my offer to walk away. This child will be raised a Ballantyne—no one will ever have to know that he, or she, is yours. I'm giving you permission to forget about this conversation."

Something flashed in Tyce's eyes. Sage tried to ignore him as he stepped up to walk beside her, a silent, brooding, sexy mass of muscle.

"We're not done discussing this, Sage," he said, his voice a low growl.

"We really are, Tyce." Sage forced the words through her tight lips. "Don't contact me again. We are over."

"Yeah, you can think that," Tyce said, standing up. "But you'd be wrong."

* * *

Little Secrets: Unexpectedly Pregnant is part of the Little Secrets series: Untamed passion, unexpected pregnancy...

Dear Reader,

The Ballantyne siblings are Manhattan royalty: successful, brilliant and pretty hot. The gems they sell are priceless but family is everything. And this one just got a little complicated!

Sage Ballantyne's family is growing rapidly. Her brothers have all found their soul mates and this is difficult for Sage, a woman determined to protect herself from love and all the forms it takes. After all, she knows what it feels like to love and then lose the people closest to you; her parents' death when she was a child ripped her apart.

As for dating and men? Well, she never gets close enough to anyone to fall in love. That's what she did with artist and sculptor Tyce Latimore. Tyce and Sage have a combustible relationship, and a chance meeting at an art gallery three years later leads to more than words flying and Sage finds herself pregnant. Cheated out of a childhood, Tyce is reclusive and broody and readily admits to being emotionally unavailable. Sage gives him the option to walk away but Tyce can't...

Tyce Latimore and the Ballantynes have unfinished business...

Love my Ballantynes! Hope you do, too!

Happy reading,

Joss

xxx

Connect with me at www.josswoodbooks.com

Twitter: @josswoodbooks

Facebook: Joss Wood Author

JOSS WOOD

———

LITTLE SECRETS:
UNEXPECTEDLY PREGNANT

Recycling programs
for this product may
not exist in your area.

ISBN-13: 978-1-335-97125-8

Little Secrets: Unexpectedly Pregnant

Copyright © 2018 by Joss Wood

Printed in U.S.A.

Joss Wood loves books and traveling—especially to the wild places of southern Africa. She has the domestic skills of a potted plant and drinks far too much coffee.

Joss has written for Harlequin KISS, Harlequin Presents and, most recently, the Harlequin Desire line. After a career in business, she now writes full-time. Joss is a member of the Romance Writers of America and Romance Writers of South Africa.

Books by Joss Wood

Harlequin Desire

Convenient Cinderella Bride

From Mavericks to Married

Trapped with the Maverick Millionaire
Pregnant by the Maverick Millionaire
Married to the Maverick Millionaire

The Ballantyne Billionaires

His Ex's Well-Kept Secret
Reunited...and Pregnant
The CEO's Nanny Affair
Little Secrets: Unexpectedly Pregnant

Visit her Author Profile page at Harlequin.com, or josswoodbooks.com, for more titles.

One

"Why does this sculpture make me think of hot, amazing, fantastic sex?"

Sage Ballantyne looked at the woman she hoped would become her sister-in-law, but didn't reply to her outrageous statement. Tyce Latimore's work, whether it was an oil painting or a wood-and-steel sculpture, always elicited a strong reaction. He was one of the best artists of his generation. Of many generations.

Thank God he was also the only artist of his generation who refused to attend his opening nights. If there had been even the slightest chance he might appear, then Sage would've stayed away.

Sage flicked her eyes over the abstract six-foot-high sculpture. It was unusual and very unlike Tyce's normally fluid lines.

"There isn't a curve in sight but it screams passion and lust," Piper said.

Sage's eyebrows lifted. "I'm not seeing what you are."

Piper pulled Sage to stand next to her.

"Try this perspective," Piper suggested, her cheeks tinged with pink.

Sage laughed at Piper's embarrassment and turned back to look at the sculpture. Actually, from this angle it did look like two people bent over a desk, and Piper was right; when you made that connection you saw the passion in the piece. This sculpture would be a talking point in his reviews. The art critics would wax eloquent about Tyce's take on human sexuality.

Sage knew how he felt about sex; he liked it. Often and any way he could get it.

"But why the frog?" Piper asked before moving on to another display.

Every muscle in Sage's body stiffened. Oh, no, he hadn't. No way, no how. Not even Tyce Latimore would have the balls to...

She looked at the sculpture again and yep, there on the "desk" was a tiny, beautifully made steel frog, its surface treated so that it took on a greenish hue. In an instant Sage flashed back to three years before.

They'd arrived separately to a party, not wanting to tip off the world about their relationship—the heiress and the hot artist, professionally and personally, would be big news—and they'd spent the evening pretending not to know each other. The tension had been hot and sexy and, by the time Tyce dropped a quick suggestion in her ear that they meet in the library, she was a vibrating, hot, sticky mess of take-me-now. Within twenty seconds of slipping into the room, the door was locked, Tyce had her dress up her hips and had stripped her of her soaking thong. He'd unzipped, leaned her over the desk and he'd taken her, hard and fast, from behind.

The jade frog on her host's desk had watched them, thoroughly unamused.

Sage hauled in a breath as her heart tried to claw its way out of her chest. How dare he? What they'd done together was not for public dissemination.

Just another reason she'd been right to walk away from him three years ago.

"That sculpture was difficult." Tyce's unmistakable deep and velvety voice came from behind her. "I was constantly distracted by the memories of that night. And others."

His words were low enough for only her to hear. She didn't turn, but she felt the heat pouring off his body and she inhaled his soapy, sexy all-man smell. Lust skittered over her. As usual, Sage felt like she'd been plugged into the nearest electrical outlet. Her skin buzzed, her heart stumbled and her mind felt off-kilter.

Three years and he still had the ability to rocket her from composed to crazy. Three years and her first instinct was to beg him to take her to bed. Three years and instead of being angry with him for depicting their encounter in the library in an, admittedly, very abstract way, she wanted to kiss him.

Or slap him…

Then, like now, he pulled her in and tempted her into edging closer. Generally, Sage found it easy to step away from men she found too attractive or too interesting. They weren't worth the hurt that was the inevitable outcome of becoming entangled in someone's life.

Determined to protect herself, Sage seldom allowed relationships, especially those with men, to deepen past a week or two. With Tyce, it had taken her six weeks to convince herself to leave. He was supremely dangerous.

Tempting, addictive… All that and more.

So, obviously, kissing him was out of the question.

Sage spun around on her ice pick heels and her hand connected with his cheek. Instantly mortified and regretful, she watched that too-handsome face harden, his obsidian eyes turn, if that was at all possible, darker. He opened his mouth to say something but instead of speaking his hands gripped her hips and he yanked her into his hard, muscled chest. His temper-tinged mouth covered hers, his hot tongue slipping between her lips, and Sage was lost, swept away to a place only Tyce could take her. Sage dug her nails into his arms, feeling his bulging muscles through the thin fabric of his black dress shirt and, wanting more, her hands skated over his broad chest, danced across those washboard abs she'd loved to tickle and taste.

Tyce lifted his mouth off hers. "Come with me."

Sage looked around for Piper, caught her eye and Piper waved her away, silently giving her permission to leave without her. She shouldn't; this really wasn't a good idea. But instead of saying no, instead of dismissing him or walking away—creating distance between herself and people was, after all, what she did best—she placed her hand in his and allowed him to lead her out of the gallery.

Tyce rolled out of his king-size bed in his borrowed apartment and headed to the luxurious en suite bathroom. Three years later and sex with Sage was still fantastic. He never had better with anyone else, he thought as he tossed the condom away. Sex had never been an issue; everything else was… Had been.

Tyce leaned forward and placed his fingers on his right cheekbone, checking for but not expecting to see finger marks from the force of Sage's hand connecting with his face ten hours before. Tyce blew out a long breath. Only they could rocket from a slap to a kiss to having wild sex all within the space of an hour. He and Sage Ballantyne were, had always been, a combustible combination. There was a reason why they'd avoided each other for three years; put them in a room together and some sort of firestorm always occurred.

Tyce gripped the edge of the vanity. Judging by her deer-in-the-headlights look when she turned around, she hadn't expected to see him at his own exhibition and he couldn't blame her. His presence last night had been an aberration. He hated discussing his work, having people fawn over him and his art. To Tyce, it was a simple equation. If you liked what he did, buy it. If not, he didn't care. There was no need to endlessly discuss his influences and inspiration for every piece. Luckily for him, art lovers seemed to connect with what he produced. His taciturn attitude to publicity and art critics and his reclusive nature added, so his agent, Tom, said, to his mystique.

He'd only gone to the exhibition because Tom insisted he meet the wealthy CEO who wanted a sculpture for the lobby of her new corporate headquarters. It was a commission that would raise the levels of his depleted coffers and it wasn't an offer he could treat lightly.

All thoughts of the commission, his agent and staying at the exhibition evaporated when he laid eyes on Sage for the first time in three years. A second after noticing her, Tyce felt his head buzzing, his skin shrinking and his world tilting. Damn; she was still as enticing and compelling and make-him-crazy as she'd been before. The world faded and he'd spun away from the CEO—who happened to be very female, very into him and very willing to give him a commission—and pushed his way through the crowds to reach her.

It was easy to call her hair black but it wasn't, not really. It was the deepest, darkest brown he'd ever seen. Her eyes were the blue of Moroccan tiles and her body a product of a lifetime spent in ballet class. Sage, damn her, was effortlessly graceful and knee-knocking sexy. She was the only woman who'd ever caused his heartbeat to spike, his lungs to contract and his brain to chant...*mine, mine, mine.* He'd been thinking of cotton sheets and a massive bed as he'd approached her and it seemed natural to open their conversation with a sexy quip. She, obviously, hadn't and responded with that furious slap. But, because he'd seen the desire in her eyes and heard her low, excited gasp as his lips met hers, he ignored his sting-ing cheek and...yeah, hell then broke loose. An hour later they were both naked and panting and pretty much stayed that way for the rest of the night. Tyce ran his hands over his face. Last night they'd let their bodies do their talking but the sun was up and real-ity was knocking on the door.

Literally. Tyce opened the door to Sage's soft rap and looked into her vivid eyes. Ballantyne eyes. She was gorgeous, Tyce thought, feeling the action down below. They'd just had rock-my-world sex for most of the night and he wanted more.

Tyce tensed, waiting for her to ask him when they'd see each other again, whether he'd call her later. He couldn't do either; there were far too many secrets between them, a history that didn't make that feasible.

"I should give you hell about that sculpture," she said, "but I don't have the energy for anything more than coffee. Too bad there isn't any. I checked. Do you actually live here?"

She posed the question as a joke but it cut too close to the bone for comfort. How would she react if he told her that he only occasionally used this Chelsea apartment belonging to his biggest client? It was easier to meet Sage in Manhattan than to explain to her, and everybody, that he, despite his sculptures and paintings selling for up to five million each, had just enough cash to keep producing his massive abstracts, to buy steel for his sculptures and to pay the mortgage and amenities on his warehouse in Brooklyn where he worked. And actually lived.

Sage waited for him to respond but when he didn't, she shrugged. "So, since you don't have the juice of life, I'm going to take off."

He wanted to protest but knew it was for the best so Tyce just nodded. After all, nothing had changed.

Sage shimmied those slim legs into a pair of designer jeans and hooked the tabs of a lilac bra together. Tyce, comfortable in his nudity, pushed his shoulder into the doorframe and watched the tension seep into her spine, into those long, toned limbs. He knew what she was thinking: How could they be so perfectly in sync between the sheets and unable to talk to each other outside the bedroom?

They'd done this before. They'd been amazing in bed but out of the bedroom they'd been useless. Used to being on his own, he'd struggled with giving equal attention to his art and to her. Art, it had to be said, always won the battle. At that time, as always, he'd needed to sell as many of his pieces as he could. But, on a more fundamental level, he knew that he had to keep his emotional distance. Relationships, with Sage or anyone else, demanded more than he had to give. His lovers objected to his need to isolate himself, to spend hours and days in his studio only coming out for food, a shower and, yeah, sex. They wanted attention, affection and he, mostly, wanted to be left alone, content to communicate through his vivid, dark oil paintings and his steel-and-wood sculptures. He wasn't good at personal connections. He'd expended all the emotional energy he'd been given caring for a depressed mother and raising his baby sister and he never again wanted to feel like he was standing on a rickety raft in a tempestuous sea. He'd held Sage at an emotional distance, unable to let her go but knowing that she needed and deserved more from him. Her adoptive father's death had been their personal tipping point. Since he couldn't see himself in a relationship, didn't want to be tied down, he'd used Connor Ballantyne's passing to put some space between them, and Sage, surprisingly, had let that happen by not trying to reconnect.

Stepping up and helping her deal with Connor's death would've flipped their relationship from casual to serious, from skimming the surface to ducking beneath the waves and he'd been too damn scared of drowning to take that risk.

Tyce rubbed his hands over his face. The Ballantyne situation was complicated—he and his sister, Lachlyn, were the only people who knew that Lachlyn was Connor Ballantyne's illegitimate daughter—and his attraction to Sage was not, had never been, helpful. His art, the paintings and the intricate sculptures, were the one thing in his life that made complete sense. He knew exactly what he was doing with his art.

Reaching back, Tyce snagged a towel from the rail and wrapped it around his hips, keeping his eyes on Sage as she pushed her feet into spiky heels. She picked up her leather bag and pulled it over her shoulder.

She pointed a finger at him. "So, I'm going to go."

Tyce saw the shimmer in her eyes that suggested tears and his heart constricted.

Hurting Sage was never what he intended to do, not now and not three years ago.

"Sage, I—" Tyce didn't complete the sentence, not sure what he was about to say. *Don't go? Thanks for a great night? Let's try again?*

Because the second thought was trite and the last impossible, he just stepped forward and when he was close enough, dropped a kiss on her temple. "Take care," he murmured.

Sage pushed the sharp tip of her fingernail into his stomach. "If I see anything in your art that references this night, I will personally disembowel you."

Not bothering to look at him again, she glided from the room, a perfect package of class and sass, her back ramrod straight.

Turning back into the bathroom, Tyce lifted his head and looked at his reflection in the mirror, unimpressed with the man looking back at him. His sister, Lachlyn, deserved to own something of the company her father, Connor, created, and in chasing down and buying Ballantyne International shares he thought he was doing the right thing, the honorable thing, but sleeping with Sage, then and now, had never been part of the plan. Originally he'd just wanted to get to know her to find out as much as he could about the iconic Manhattan family because he'd intended to use that knowledge to his, or Lachlyn's, advantage.

He hadn't banked on their chemistry, on the desire that flared between them. He'd thought that she would be easy to walk away from once they got each other out of their systems, but that had proved to be more difficult than he thought. Last night had blown those preconceptions out of the window. For as long as he lived he'd crave Sage Ballantyne...

As fast as a snakebite, Tyce's fist slammed into the mirror above his head and glass flew from the frame and dropped into the basin, onto the floor. Tyce looked at his ultra-distorted reflection in the thin shards that remained in the frame and nodded, satisfied.

That looked far more like the person he knew himself to be.

Two

Three months later...

"Are you going to slap me again?"

"The night is still young, who knows?"

Tyce slid onto the barstool next to Sage, ordered a whiskey from the bartender and looked at his former lover. She'd pulled her long, normally curly hair into a sleek tail, allowing her eyes to dominate her face. Tonight her irises were periwinkle blue surrounded with a navy ring; they could be, depending on her mood, navy, denim or that unusual shade of Moroccan blue.

Her eyes always, every single time, had the ability to drop him to his knees. God had not been playing fair when he'd combined an amazing set of blues with a face that was near perfect—heart shaped, high cheekbones, sexy mouth, stubborn chin—and then, just for kicks, placed that head on top of a body that was naturally lean, intensely feminine, all sexy.

He loved her face, he loved her body and God knew that he loved making love to her, with her… He wanted to kiss that mouth, suck on her skin, allow his hands to stroke that endlessly creamy, warm, fragrant skin.

It had been so damn long and, after three years of sheer hell, one night with her had been like offering a dehydrated man a drop of water. He wanted her legs wrapped around his hips, to hear her soft moans in his ear, his tongue in that hot, sweet mouth.

Sage had no idea that his pants were tighter and that his lungs were battling to take in air. She just took a sip of her drink and wrinkled her nose in a way he'd always found adorable. "I suppose I should apologize for slapping you but the incident made all the social columns, creating more publicity for your already successful exhibition and sending your already overinflated prices sky-high."

Overinflated? Tyce winced and then shrugged. It wasn't like he hadn't had the same thought a time or two. The prices his art commanded were ridiculous; it wasn't like he was a modern-day Picasso or Rembrandt. He was just a guy who slapped steel and wood together, tossed paint onto a canvas in a way people seemed to like. Art critics, his agent and the gallery owners would be shocked if they ever found out how little effort went into the art they all revered.

No one knew or suspected that most of his time was spent painting intensely detailed portraits that were accurate to the last brushstroke. His portraits, intimate, honest, time and blood sucking, were where he found and lost himself. Many of those never-seen portraits were of Sage, and Tyce neither knew or cared to speculate what that meant.

Silence fell between them and Tyce looked around the room. He'd been surprised to receive a text from Sage inviting him to attend the Ballantyne cocktail party and jewelry exhibition and there had never been any doubt that he'd go. Firstly, if one was personally invited to look at one of the best collections of fantastically rare and ridiculously expensive jewelry one took the opportunity. He also wanted to look at the new line Sage designed and it was, as he expected, fabulous. Whimsical but modern, feminine but strong…so Sage. And because he was a guy he was hoping that Sage's request to meet would lead to some head-bangin', bed-breaking sex.

There was only one way to find out. "So, is this a booty call?"

Sage blinked. "What?"

"Did you ask to meet so that we can hook up again?"

"You arrogant jerk!" Her eyes sparked with irritation and color seeped into her face. "Are you insane?"

Probably. And, if he was, then her incredible eyes and rocking body and the memories of how good they were together were to blame.

"So, you didn't call me to try and talk me into

a night of hot sex?" Tyce didn't have to pretend to sound disappointed; the memories of touching, tasting, loving Sage kept him up most nights. He wished he could ring-fence his thoughts so that he only remembered her scent, her soft, creamy skin and the taste on his tongue. But, unfortunately, his mind always wandered off into dangerous territory—how it would feel to wake up to her face in the morning, to hear her soft *good night* before he slept. He only allowed himself the briefest of fantasies about what a life spent with Sage would look like before he vaporized those thoughts.

Sage was part of a dynamic, successful family and he wasn't referring to the immense Ballantyne wealth. Sage and her brothers knew what family meant, how to be part of one.

He didn't have a cookin' clue. The Ballantyne family, from what he understood, worked as a well-oiled machine, each part of that machine different but essential to the process.

Tyce had been the engine that powered his family along—an engine constantly on the point of breaking down. He'd done his best to provide what Lachlyn needed but had been so damn busy trying to survive that he emotionally neglected his sister. Sage's life partner would be an emotionally intelligent dude, would be able to slide into the Ballantyne family and know how to be, act, respond… The man who she married would know how to deal with and contribute to the clan.

Tyce wasn't that man. He'd never be that man and

it was stupid to spend more than a minute thinking that he could be.

So, when he'd seen her text message asking him to meet tonight, he'd jumped to the only conclusion that made sense, that she wanted another hookup. During his shower he'd fantasized about how he would take her... Fast or slow? Her on top or him? Either way, the only thing that was nonnegotiable was that he'd be looking in her eyes when she shattered, wanting to see if she needed him as much as he needed her.

Instead of looking soft and dreamy, her eyes blazed with pure blue anger. Right, real life...

"No, Tyce, I didn't call you because I wanted hot sex." Sage answered him in a dry, sarcastic voice.

Tyce took a sip of his whiskey, the urge to tease fleeing. Did she suddenly look nervous? He lifted his eyebrows until Sage spoke. "But I did—do—have something to tell you."

Tyce looked around the room while he rubbed his jaw, his gut screaming that whatever she had to say was going to rock his world. He didn't want his world rocked, he just wanted to either have sex with Sage or to go home and paint. Since sex wasn't happening, he itched to slap oil onto canvas, eager to work his frustration out with slashes of indigo and Indian red, manganese violet and magenta. "Just spit it out and get it done." Tyce snapped out the words, his tone harsh.

Sage blew air out over her lips and briefly closed her eyes. When they opened again, he saw her resolve. And when she finally formed the words, they shifted his world.

"I don't expect anything from you, not money or time or involvement. But you should know that I am pregnant and the baby is yours."

Tyce was still trying to make sense of her words, trying to decipher them, when Sage placed a swift, final kiss to the left of his mouth. "Goodbye, Tyce. It was…fun. Except when it wasn't."

Sage, having said what she needed to, took advantage of his astonishment and stood up. She was about to pick up her clutch and leave when his hand shot out and gripped her wrist.

When she looked at him she noticed that his eyes were pure black fire. "Sit. Stay."

Those eyes, God, they still had the power to dissolve her knees. Eyes of a warrior, Sage thought. Because he made her feel off-kilter, she handed him a cool look. "I am not a puppy you are trying to train."

Tyce gripped his nose with his thumb and forefinger. "God, Sage, just give me a sec, okay? You've just told me that you're pregnant. I need a goddamn minute! So, yeah, sit your ass down, okay?"

Hearing the note of panic in Tyce's voice, Sage slid back onto the high barstool and crossed her legs. She listened as Tyce ordered another whiskey from the bartender and watched the color seep slowly back into his face.

"We need to…" she began.

Tyce shook his head and held up his hand to stop her talking. "Another drink and some more time."

Sage nodded and leaned back in her chair, a little relieved that she'd told him, that it was finally done. It had taken every gram of courage she possessed to send that text message asking him to meet, and she'd known that he'd think she was looking for another one-night stand. Could she blame him? Their entire relationship had been based around their physical attraction and he was a guy... Of course he'd think she just wanted sex.

But their crazy chemistry had led to a very big consequence...

Sage rolled her head, trying to loosen the tension in her neck. She'd sit here, let him take the time he needed for the news to sink in and after what she hoped would be a drama-free conversation, she'd leave. Then she could put him and their brief roller coaster—What should she call it? Fling? Affair? Madness?—behind her.

God, though it had been brief, their time together had been intense. They'd met at the opening of a small gallery around the corner from her apartment and the attraction between them sizzled. Sage would like to blame that on his mixed heritage, Korean and French, on his dark Asian eyes, square chin and blinding smile, and his tall, muscled body. But she'd grown up surrounded by good-looking men and looks didn't impress her much. No, it was Tyce's stillness, his control and his aura of elusiveness, and unavailability, that attracted her.

Tyce had told her, straight up and straightaway, that he wanted to sleep with her but that he wasn't the settle-down, buy-her-flowers type. They could hang, enjoy each other, but she shouldn't expect anything more from him. She appreciated his up-front attitude and it soon dawned on her that she was drawn to a younger, darker, less chatty version of her beloved uncle Connor. Connor had been utterly devoted to his adopted kids, had looked after his employees and had been a hardworking, focused businessman, but a monogamous, committed relationship never featured on Connor's list of priorities. Trying to pin men like Connor and Tyce down was like trying to capture smoke in a sieve.

And maybe she'd found Tyce a little more attractive because she knew he would never offer her the very thing that scared her the most: an emotionally intimate relationship. She'd been the apple of her parents' eye, the baby girl who had her entire family wrapped around her finger, loved and adored until she woke up one morning and heard that the biggest part of her life was gone and wasn't ever coming back.

She'd avoided relationships outside of the people who lived in Connor's iconic brownstone fondly referred to as The Den—her brothers, Connor, and Jo, Linc's mom and the woman Connor hired to help him raise three orphans. She had girlfriends she enjoyed but whom she kept at an arm's length, and she wasn't much of a dater.

Tyce had been hard to resist. Sage had been in

love with his art for years. His work was detailed and exquisite, full of angst and emotion. From their first meeting, admiration and attraction swirled and whirled and she'd quickly said yes when he suggested dinner. They didn't make it to a restaurant; instead they'd tumbled into bed and Sage finally understood the power of addiction. She craved Tyce with a ferocity that scared her.

After six weeks of fantastic sex, Sage realized she was on the brink of falling in love with Tyce and couldn't, wouldn't allow that to happen. Terrified, she did what she did best, she made plans to run and immediately booked a ticket to Hong Kong, telling her brothers that their Asian clients needed her attention. The day before her scheduled flight to Asia, Connor passed away and her entire world changed. Connor's death allowed her to put the distance between her and Tyce she'd been seeking with her trip to Hong Kong.

And Connor's death reminded her of why it was better to keep her distance from people and that she was wise to avoid emotional and intimate relationships. It hurt too damn much when the people she loved left her life.

She had enough people to love, enough people to worry about. And now—Sage placed her hand on her stomach—she had a baby on the way, a little person who would become the center of her world. Her baby, she ruefully admitted, was one person she had no choice but to love, someone she couldn't push away.

Well played, Universe.

What did having a baby mean to Tyce? Sage wanted to ask him but, judging from his give-me-space expression, he wouldn't answer her. Would he walk? Would he want to be involved? If he wanted contact with his child, how would that work? What if he wanted to co-parent? What then? When she'd texted him she'd been consumed by the idea of telling him, needing to get the dreaded deed done. She hadn't thought beyond that. Well, she had thought about how sexy he was and how much she wanted to make love to him again…

Like those thoughts were productive. Besides, them going to bed was exactly what led to their current predicament. Then again, one couldn't fall pregnant twice. *Jeez, Sage, pull yourself together, woman!*

Tyce abruptly stood up, nearly tipping his barstool with the force of his movement. "I need to get out of here."

"Okay, well…" Sage bit her bottom lip and looked around. "Give me a call if you want to chat about this some more."

Tyce looked like a hard-assed warrior about to go to battle. "Oh, hell, no, we're leaving together."

Sage frowned at his high-handed comment. She wasn't ready to leave. This cocktail party and exhibition of the Ballantyne family jewelry collection was the culmination of their latest PR campaign to attract new customers. Her family was all in attendance and she was expected to stick around. Not that anyone would notice if she left… Her brothers Jaeger and Beck were both slow dancing with their women—Piper and Cady—and she was the last thing on their minds. Her oldest brother, Linc, who'd brought Tate, his son's temporary nanny, to the party, was nowhere to be seen.

Sage was sure that she could leave and no one would be any wiser but that would mean leaving with Tyce and that wasn't an option. "I don't think so."

"Walk out with me or I swear, I'll toss you over my shoulder and walk you out that way."

His alpha bossiness only turned her on when they were naked but since they weren't—and would never be again—his terse tone ticked her off. She opened her mouth to blast him and closed it again at the determination in his eyes. She could either leave walking or over his shoulder and she didn't want a scene to ruin this fabulous evening. Sage glared at him, picked up her designer clutch and walked with him into the foyer of the ballroom. She collected her coat and went to stand by the elevators.

The doors opened, Sage followed Tyce into the cube and pushed the button for the first floor. As the doors closed, the spacious interior shrunk with a big, broad, freaked-out man inside.

Tyce slapped his hand against the emergency stop button.

"What the hell, Sage? You're pregnant?"

Obviously, he was taking some time to process the news. Sage winced at his shout, his words bouncing off the wood paneling. She lifted her hands as the elevator shuddered to a stop.

"Okay, calm down, Tyce."

Pathetic as it was, it was all she could think of to say. Even furious, he was ludicrously good-looking. Blue-black hair cut stylishly with short back and sides, equally dark eyebrows over those black sultry eyes. When he smiled, which was, in her opinion, far too rarely, he could charm birds down from trees, criminals into converting and start polar caps melting. Sage wished that she could say Tyce Latimore was just a pretty face but he was so much more than that. He was tall, a few inches above six foot and his body, that body she'd licked and explored and teased and tasted, was all muscle honed from a lifetime dedicated to martial arts. Tae Kwon Do, judo, Krav Maga…they'd all contributed to creating a body that was spectacular and spectacularly sexy. The hair on her arms lifted and her fingers ached to touch him. Her off-the-shoulder silk dress felt abrasive against her sensitive skin and want and need danced through her.

Focus, Sage. Sheesh.

Tyce pushed his jacket back to place his hands on his hips, his expression summer-storm vicious. "Are you messing with me?"

Sage just barely restrained herself from rolling her eyes at his question.

"Yeah, Tyce," she sarcastically muttered. "I crave your attention that much that I'd make up a story like this to play games with your head!" Seeing his still skeptical face, she shook her head and, needing support, she leaned her back against the wall of the elevator. "I am pregnant. Since you're the only guy I've slept with in the three months—" Three years, she mentally corrected, but she wasn't telling him that! "—I think it's safe to assume that the kid is yours."

"But we used condoms," Tyce said, pushing his shaking hands into his hair.

Sage blushed. "That first time…you did slide in without a condom. You put one on later but maybe…" Lord, this was embarrassing! "…something slipped past."

Tyce stared at her, his hands linked behind his head and his expression stricken with panic and fear. "I can't be a father, Sage. I don't want to be a father. I don't want kids!"

Sage assumed as much.

Sage reached around him to release the emergency stop button. "As I told you, that's not a problem. I don't expect anything from you. You can carry on living your life as you always have."

"You can't do this on your own!" he said and for the first time ever Sage saw Tyce a little unhinged. He banged his fist against the stop button to prevent it from going any farther and the car's shudder reverberated through her.

"I am young, healthy, have huge family support and ample resources to hire the help I need to raise this child," Sage told him, pushing a finger into his chest. "I don't need anything from you."

A little support would be nice, a kind word, but wishing for either was futile. Tyce wasn't the kind, supportive type. Hot and hard, amazing, fantastic sex? Yes. Warm and reassuring? No. She'd only told him because he had the right to know and not because she expected anything from him. She didn't want anything from him…or from any other man.

She was fine, *safe*, on her own.

"Miss Ballantyne?" Sage jumped at the disembodied voice coming from a speaker above her head. "Is everything alright in there?"

She nodded at the camera in the top corner of the elevator. "Everything is fine, thank you. We're just having a chat."

Chat? They were having a life-changing conversation. There was nothing *chatty* about it.

"Okay then." The voice sounded dubious. "Um? Do you think you could, um, chat somewhere else? There are people waiting for the elevator."

Sage nodded, walked to stand between Tyce and the light panel and pushed the emergency stop again. She pulled in a large breath and turned to face Tyce, who was staring down at the mulberry-colored carpet. "Tyce."

He didn't lift his head, so Sage called his name again. He eventually looked at her with those intensely dark, pain-filled eyes.

"I'm letting you off the hook. Look, I'm presuming that your statement from three years ago—when you told me that you don't do commitment—still holds?"

"Yeah." It was a small word but a powerful response.

Sage nodded. "I'm very okay with that—I'm not

looking for someone to nest with me. Take my offer to walk away. This child will be raised a Ballantyne. No one will ever have to know that he, or she, is yours. I'm giving you permission to forget about this conversation."

Something flashed in Tyce's eyes and Sage frowned, not sure what she'd seen. Before she could say any more, the doors to the elevator opened and they faced a bank of people waiting for the tardy lift. Sage pulled on her practiced, cool smile and stepped into the throng. She swiftly walked into the lobby and she nodded when the concierge asked her whether she wanted a taxi. Sage pulled on her coat and tried to ignore Tyce as he stepped up to walk beside her, a silent, brooding sexy mass of muscle.

She'd barely stepped onto the curb when a taxi pulled up and the doorman hurried to open the door. Sage climbed inside and sighed when Tyce crouched in the space between the open car door and her seat.

"We're not done discussing this, Sage," he said, his voice a low growl.

"We really are, Tyce." Sage forced the words through her tight lips. "Don't contact me again. We are over."

"Yeah, you can think that," Tyce said, standing up. "But you'd be wrong."

The slam of the taxi door was an exclamation point at the end of his sentence.

Three

In his converted warehouse in Brooklyn, Tyce stood at the massive windows that provided perfect light for his studio, his forearm resting on the glass. He'd been home an hour and he was grateful that he'd fought the impulse to follow Sage to her apartment. Instead of acting impetuously, he'd fought his way through the shock to slow his thoughts down, to think this situation through. He needed time to let the fact that he was going to be a dad sink in, to figure this out.

Tyce walked away from the window to the far wall, to a row of canvases that were stacked against the wall. Sitting cross-legged on the paint splattered floor, he reached for the most recent canvas, a portrait of Sage at her workbench, her brow furrowed in concentration, a pencil in her hand. He'd painted the portrait from a photo published in an arts magazine and it was, he admitted, as lifelike as the photo. Bending his knees, Tyce stared at the canvas, thinking that his child was growing her belly, that his DNA was joining with hers to create a new life.

God, what an awesome, terrifying, crazy thought. What the hell did Life think it was doing, asking him—the most emotionally disconnected person on the planet—to be a father? As a child he'd been consumed by anxiety, responsibility, overwhelmed by a world that asked him to deal with far too much, far too soon. Adulthood, his and Lachlyn's, and his mother's death, allowed him some measure of relief. But, because he never wanted to feel so unbalanced—*scared*—again he deliberately distanced himself from emotionally investing in situations and people because that would make him vulnerable. To Tyce it was a simple situation, vulnerability equaled hurt and pain was to be avoided. The logical conclusion was to avoid emotion altogether, like he had with Sage three years ago, or to disconnect, like he had learned to do with his mother.

Tyce supposed that, to the world, he looked normal, content, like he had it all. Nobody knew, not even Lachlyn, that on the inside, he felt hollow and empty. Kicking the crap out of his sparring partner at the dojo and pushing his body to the limit made him feel alive but the endorphins soon wore off. Art, mostly, provided a distraction and he, occasionally, felt the hit of adrenaline when he painted his oils or constructed his sculptures. Mostly he found the process easy and intellectually undemanding.

Tyce tipped his head back. Instead of seeing paint-streaked wooden beams and the steel pipes that were a feature of his converted warehouse he saw the faded walls of the small, two-bedroom apartment he'd lived in for most of his life. He was sitting on the cold floor outside his mother's bedroom door, rocking a crying Lachlyn, wishing that his mother would unlock the door and tell him that she was okay. That they'd be okay. He'd always wondered what he was doing wrong, why his mother needed to hide from him and his sister. He remembered the hundreds of drawings he did for her, hoping that, maybe once, she'd acknowledge his effort, desperate for any attention from her.

His index finger traced the line of Sage's jaw. At one time selling portraits—quick charcoal or ink sketches—had kept the roof over their heads, food in the fridge. In his early teens he'd sold rough sketches on street corners and in Central Park and later he sold his sketches to the women attending the art classes where he posed, naked, as an artist's model.

He clearly remembered feeling anxious as his hand flew over the paper, working out how much he could charge, how many sketches he needed to do to cover the latest unexpected expense; a kid struggling to gather rent money. Eventually he managed to control the anxiety, the burning resentment, and he'd learned to do that by detaching. From things, from the need for support and affirmation and, eventually, from people. Sage was the only person who'd ever threatened his control, who tempted him to edge closer, to climb into her head and let her climb into his. He couldn't do that, wouldn't allow himself to open up again.

And her being such a temptation was exactly why he'd allowed her to walk away from him years ago, why he'd let her slip through his fingers. It had been self-preservation in action.

He'd been an adult all his life, had dealt with situations no child should have to, had raised his sister as best he could. He wasn't scared of much but, God, Sage having a baby terrified him. Tyce linked his arms around his bent knees, as fear, hot and acidic, bubbled in a space just under his heart. And, like it or not, he and Sage were now joined together in an age-old way, through the mingling of their DNA. No matter how Tyce looked at it, as the mother of his child, Sage would be a permanent fixture in his life. Sage was also the only person who'd ever come close to cracking his armor and that meant that she was desperately dangerous.

He didn't like it but the situation couldn't be changed and all he could do was manage the process. How to do that? Tyce stood up and walked over to his desk in the corner of the studio, pulling out his battered office chair and dropping into it. First things first… Since he was going to be connected to the Ballantyne family for a long time to come, he had to come clean. About everything. First to Sage, then to her brothers.

And yeah, that was going to be as much fun as running around outside, naked, on a winter's night in Siberia. But it couldn't be avoided and it had to be done, and soon.

Sage, resentful that she'd been pulled away from her workbench to attend a meeting at Ballantyne International headquarters, stepped out of the elevator and immediately turned left, waving to the staff working behind the glass walls that were a feature of the Ballantyne corporate offices. Sage deeply appreciated the people who worked for their company, each one an essential cog to keep the massive organization running smoothly. She knew enough about business to contribute to the partners' meetings but she trusted her brothers to run the company, just as they trusted her to translate their rich clients' vague desires for "something special" into works of gemstone art.

But occasionally, as a full partner of Ballantyne International, she was expected to attend the meetings Linc called. She'd reluctantly shrug out of her work clothes—comfortable jeans and loose tops—and change into something more businesslike; today's outfit was a red-and-pink geometric top and plain black wool pants worn over two-inch-heeled boots. Her makeup consisted of a swipe of nude lipstick and she'd pulled her hair into a long braid.

She had the jewelry-designer-to-Ballantyne-partner switch down to a fine art.

At the end of the hallway, Sage pushed open the

glass door to Amy's office, thankful to see the PA Linc and Beck shared at her desk, laconically typing on her computer. The walls to the offices on either side of Amy's desk were opaque and Sage couldn't tell whether Linc and Beck were in their respective offices or not.

"Why is your phone off?" Amy demanded, looking at her over the frames of her trendy glasses. "FYI, smoke signals are notoriously unreliable these days."

Knowing that underneath Amy's glossy and sarcastic shell was a gooey center, Sage leaned across her desk to drop a kiss on her cheek. "Sorry I worried you."

"I nearly came to your place myself. I hate it when you don't answer your phone." Amy pushed her chair away from her desk, her eyes brightening. "So, what do you think about Linc and Tate's engagement? Isn't it fabulous?"

Sure, her life was in turmoil but Sage was genuinely happy for her brothers. Linc and Tate aside, there was more good news: Piper and Jaeger were expecting twin boys, Tate was going to adopt Linc's son, Shaw, and Linc was going to adopt Ellie, Tate's ward and niece. Beckett was going to raise Cady's still-baking baby as his own. Sage felt no surprise at Beckett's generous offer; in the Ballantyne family blood was a nebulous concept.

Love…love always trumped DNA.

"Are you okay? You seem anxious and stressed."

As she always did, Sage shook her head and, wanting to distract Amy, ran her finger over the open face of a rose, bending down to inhale the subtle scent. "A gift from Jules?" Sage asked, thinking of Julie, Amy's soon-to-be wife.

Amy smiled softly. "Yeah. She's better at romance than I am."

Between her brothers and Amy, she was the only one with no interest in the concept. Besides, she had far more pressing problems than romance—or the lack of it in her life—she was pregnant and only Tyce knew. And, speaking of her baby's daddy, she couldn't keep ignoring his calls and messages. They'd have to talk sometime soon...

When their baby was old enough for college?

Sage pulled a face at her silliness. She'd spent two weeks with her head in the sand; she couldn't keep it there much longer. When this meeting was over she'd invite Tyce to her apartment for a chat. No, not her apartment, that was too intimate a space, too revealing. And her bed was up a short flight of stairs, above her sitting area. She'd spend the entire time looking at his mouth and hoping that he'd put her out of her misery and kiss her. His mouth had always been her downfall; their lips would touch and she'd immediately feel he was stripping her soul of all its barriers.

The fantasy was both wildly exciting and intensely dangerous and that was why she should keep the man out of her private spaces—her apartment, her body, her heart—and meet him in a public venue.

After they'd thrashed out where they stood, what they wanted, what their expectations were, she'd tell her brothers and the rest of the family about the pregnancy.

It was a plan with a hundred holes in it but it was, at least, a plan.

Amy looked at the massive clock on the wall behind Sage. "You need to move or else you're going to be late for your meeting."

"What's this meeting about, by the way?"

"I don't know." Amy frowned, looking displeased. She loathed being outside the loop. "I know nothing except that the meeting is in Connor's boardroom."

Sage turned around slowly, her eyes wide. Connor's boardroom was a little-known boardroom on the top floor of the Ballantyne building. It was only accessible by an elevator within the iconic jewelry store, Ballantyne's on Fifth, on the ground floor of this building or by a nondescript steel door at the back of the building. The room was used for very high-profile clients who demanded anonymity, buyers and sellers of gems who demanded that their movements not be brought to public attention. Or any attention at all.

Sage frowned, realizing that she had to head downstairs, enter the store and then use the elevator. It was a pain in her ass and she was guaranteed to be late.

"Dammit."

Waving a quick goodbye at Amy, Sage headed back to the private elevator that would take her directly into the back rooms of Ballantyne's on Fifth.

As she stepped into the hallway, Sage tossed a look over her shoulder and saw Amy standing behind her desk, still looking worried. Worried and hurt. It was an expression she'd seen on many faces over the years and she felt the familiar stab of guilt-slicked pain.

Amy hated that Sage kept her arm's length but it wasn't personal, she kept everyone there, except, possibly, Linc. At the age of six she'd experienced a double whammy, the deaths of both her parents. So, really, was it any surprise that her biggest fear was that she'd lose anyone she loved, that she would be left alone? Her rationale at six still made sense to her: the more distance she kept between her and the ones she loved, the less it would hurt when they went away.

Sage fully accepted that life was a series of changes, that people came and went and that life required a series of emotional shifts. Loved ones, sadly, died. Friends moved away. Relationships broke up. They all came with their own measure of pain but Sage was very sure that she never wanted to be left behind again and it was easier to walk away than stand still and endure the emotional fallout.

Sage hauled in a deep breath. Her childhood had shaped who she was today. She looked after, as much as she could, the relationships she couldn't walk away from—her brothers, their partners and Amy—but she didn't actively seek new people to add to the small circle of people she loved to distraction. She dated casually, not allowing herself to fall in love. If she did find herself someone she liked, re-ally, really liked, she never allowed the relationship to dip beneath the surface because she could never be sure of who would stay or who would go so she made it easy and pushed them all away. Somewhere between her sixth and seventh birthday she'd real-ized that it was easier to retreat from people and sit-uations than to give them a chance.

Pushing people away, creating distance, it was her thing.

Tyce was the easiest and most difficult person she'd ever walked away from. Easy because she knew that he didn't want anything serious from her, difficult because she'd been so very close to throw-ing her innate caution and self-preservation to the wind. He'd tempted her to try, to see what the hype about relationships and commitment was all about, to take a risk. Already teetering, if Tyce had given her the smallest sliver of encouragement, she might have toppled into love. But he hadn't and she did what she did best; she'd walked away.

And he'd let her.

Sage shook her head, annoyed with her thoughts. She was focusing on the past and she wasn't going in that direction. Tyce might be the father of her child and she might be crazy, fiercely attracted to him but, baby or not, she intended to keep him on the periph-ery of her life.

She did, however, have to find another way to interact with him because—she glanced down at the screen of her cell phone showing the number of calls she'd missed from Tyce—he wasn't going away.

Sage stepped out of the elevator into the back room of the original Ballantyne jewelry store and smiled at an employee who was on her way to the break room. Stepping across the hallway, she punched in the code to access the private elevator that would take her up to the secret room on the top floor of the building, adjacent to rooms holding the safes and hundreds of millions of dollars' worth of precious gems.

Sage bit her bottom lip, resigning herself to the inevitable. When this secretive meeting was over, she'd call Tyce and set up a time to meet, to discuss how involved he wanted to be in the baby's life, how they were going to deal with each other when the baby arrived. She would be cool, calm and collected. She wouldn't lose her temper or slap or kiss him.

Sage stepped into the small boardroom. Her stomach immediately rebelled at the smell of coffee rolling toward her and she frantically looked around for a trash can or a receptacle in case her morning sickness turned nasty.

A hand on her back steadied her. Sage slowly lifted her eyes to look into that familiar face, the high cheekbones, the stubble covering his strong jaw. Hard, black eyes. "You okay?" Tyce asked her, holding her biceps in a firm grip. He'd catch her if she fell, Sage thought, relieved. If her knees gave way she wouldn't hit the floor.

"What are you doing here?" she whispered, wondering if she'd dropped down Alice's rabbit hole.

An indefinable emotion flashed in Tyce's eyes. "Now that's a long story. Take a seat and we'll get into it."

Four

Tyce guided Sage to a chair and stepped away from the table, deliberately walking over to the far side of the room and leaning his shoulder into the wall, crossing his feet at the ankle. It was an insolent pose, a deliberate maneuver to keep the Ballantyne men off-balance. Tyce had deliberately dressed down for this meeting; he wore faded, paint-splattered jeans over flat-heeled boots and a clean black button-down shirt over a black T-shirt, cuffs rolled back. Linc and Beck were dressed in designer suits; Jaeger was a little less formal in suit pants and a pale cream sweater.

Sage, well, Sage looked stunning in the clashing colors of pink and red, most of her hair in a messy knot on top of her head, tendrils framing her face and falling down the back of her neck. She was innately stylish, yet people assumed it took her hours to look so perfectly put-together, but he'd seen Sage on the move; she could shove her hair up in thirty seconds, could dress in another minute. Sage wasn't one for spending hours in front of a mirror.

Tyce looked at her face and frowned at the blue stripes under her eyes, at the pallor in her skin. She looked like she'd dropped weight and it was weight she could ill afford. She kept sucking her bottom lip between her teeth, darting anxious looks at his face. Tyce, deliberately, kept his expression blank, his face a mask. She could've avoided this meeting, he reminded himself; she could've taken one of his many calls; they could've done this differently. But, after trying to reach her for two weeks, her refusal to see him or talk to him limited his options so he contacted Linc and convinced him that a meeting would be beneficial to all parties.

Tyce watched as Linc stepped forward and placed both his hands on Sage's shoulders, his gentle squeeze conveying his support. Jaeger and Beck flanked Sage on either side, arms folded and jaws tense. Her brothers were very protective of their sister and he hoped that this conversation wouldn't turn physical but who the hell knew? When you were dealing with family and money and business, anything could happen.

"Since you asked for this meeting, Latimore, would you like to get the party started?" Linc asked, his voice as cold as a subzero fridge.

Tyce nodded, straightened and walked to the table,

pulling out a chair at the head, another deliberate gesture. It was a silent *screw you* to their pecking order, telling Linc and his brothers that he wasn't going to neatly slot into their order of command.

Tyce rested his forearms on the table. He turned his head to look at Sage and wished that they were alone, that he could kiss her luscious mouth, trace the fine line of her jaw, kiss his way down her long neck to her shoulders. Peel her clothes from her body...

Tyce sighed. He was imagining Sage naked because, yeah, *that* was helpful. He ran his hand across his face and caught Sage's eye.

"This could've gone differently, Sage. If you had taken my calls, answered my emails, had a goddamn conversation with me, I wouldn't have had to do it like this."

Ignoring her frown, Tyce reached across the table and pulled his folder toward him. He flipped open the cover and withdrew a sheaf of papers and tossed them in Linc's general direction. "Share certificates showing that Lach-Ty owns around fifteen percent of Ballantyne's."

Four backs straightened, four jaws tensed. Linc picked up the share certificates, examined them and carefully placed them facedown on the table. "Would you care to explain," he asked in a dangerous-as-hell voice, "why you own fifteen percent of our company?"

Sure, that was why he was here, after all. "Technically, I don't own the shares. I just paid for them."

Linc gripped the table, his hands and knuckles

white. "Then who does own the shares and why the hell did you pay for them?"

"My sister owns those shares because I thought it was right that she owned a percentage of the company her father left to you." Tyce hesitated and thought that he might as well get it all out there so that they could move forward from a basis of truth. "I thought that, since your sister is carrying my baby, it was time to lay my cards on the table."

And that, Tyce thought, his eyes moving from one shocked Ballantyne to another, was how you dropped a bombshell.

Shock, horror, surprise, anger…all the emotions he expected were in their faces, coating their questions, their shouted demands for more information. Tyce ignored them and kept his gaze focused on Sage, who stared at him with hellfire in her eyes.

She half stood, slapped her palms on the table and leaned toward him. "How dare you tell them without my permission?"

Tyce held her gaze and lifted one shoulder in a shrug. "Because if I left it up to you, then you'd be ready to go into labor and you'd still be hemming and hawing about how to tell them, what to tell and whether you should."

"You had no right—"

Tyce pointed at her stomach. "That's my child in there too and, might I remind you, if you'd agreed to meet with me instead of ignoring me, then we could've resolved this and more."

"More? What are you talking about?" Sage demanded, her voice vibrating with fear and concern.

Linc placed a hand on Sage's shoulder and urged her back into the chair. "He's talking about the shares and alluding to Connor having a daughter."

"What? Connor never had any children," Sage emphatically stated. "That's crazy!"

"You're pregnant?" Jaeger yelled.

"Everyone shut up!" Linc ordered and looked at Sage. "Let's finish with Latimore first. Then he can get out of our hair and we can talk about your baby," Linc added in his CEO-everyone-must-listen-to-me voice. Yeah, well, Tyce didn't have to.

"Your optimism is amusing, Linc," Tyce drawled. "It's my baby too and, sorry to disappoint you, but I'm going to be around for a hell of a long time."

"No, you're not," Sage stated.

"Oh, honey, I so am. But we'll discuss that later," Tyce said, his voice quiet but holding no trace of doubt.

"Why would you think that your sister is Connor's daughter?" Linc asked, his jaw rock tight with annoyance.

"I don't *think* she is Connor's daughter, I know she is," Tyce replied. Tyce saw that they were going to argue and lifted his hand. "Look, let me start at the beginning and I'll talk you through it."

Where to start? As he said, at the beginning. Well, at Lachlyn's beginning, not his. They didn't need to know about his childhood, about those dark and dismal years before, and after, Lachlyn came along. As quickly and concisely as he could, Tyce recounted the facts. His mom had worked as a night cleaner at Ballantyne International, in this very building—something he had no reason to feel ashamed of; it was honest work and if the Ballantynes were too snobby to understand that, to hell with them—and, because Connor worked long hours, they struck up a friendship. His mom and stepdad separated, she and Connor started an affair and she became pregnant.

"My mom knew that she had no future with Connor so she went back to my stepfather hoping that he'd raise Lachlyn as his."

His stepdad, originally from Jamaica, took one look at Lachlyn, a blond-haired, blue-eyed baby, and lost his temper. Tyce took his disappearance that same day as a firm *no* on the raising-and-supporting-Lachlyn question. Those months following his stepfather's disappearance had been, by far, the worst of his life. His mom sunk into what he now knew to be postpartum depression, made a hundred times worse by her normal, run-of-the-mill depression. Looking after the baby had been a struggle for her. She hadn't had any energy left over for a confused eight-year-old boy.

"Did your mother ever tell Connor that he had a daughter?" Beck asked, his voice laced with skepticism.

"No," Tyce snapped back, frustrated. "Since Lachlyn's birth certificate states that my stepdad is her father, she didn't have a legal leg to stand on. She assumed that Connor would dismiss her claims."

"Which is exactly what we are going to do," Linc told him, his blue eyes hard.

Linc reacted exactly as he expected him to so Tyce wasn't particularly surprised. "You can, but it won't make any difference to my plans."

Tyce ran his hand around his neck, hoping to rub away the headache at the base of his skull. He darted a look at Sage and saw that her face was even whiter than before and her big, endlessly blue eyes were dark with pain and confusion. She looked like he'd punched her in the gut. The fight immediately went out of Tyce and he moved his hand across the table to cover hers. He desperately wanted to scoop her up, soothe away her pain, assure her that everything would be okay.

But Tyce, more than most, knew that life had a nebulous concept of fairness and had a shoddy record at doling out good luck.

Sage snatched her hand out from under his, as if he were contagious with some flesh-eating disease. She folded her arms against her chest and glared at him. He couldn't help his smile.

"You should know that your prissy, 'I'm a princess and you're a peasant' look turns me on."

His comment also had the added bonus of pissing her brothers off. Score.

Sage lifted her hand, her lips thinning. "This is business so let's keep it to that, okay? You and I have nothing to say to each other."

Oh, they so did. "We have a great deal to say to

one another and we will," Tyce promised her, lowering his voice.

"In your dreams, hotshot," Sage retorted, fire in her eyes.

Tyce reached across the table and pushed a curl out of her eyes with the tip of his finger. "You can fight this, kick and claw and scratch, but you and me, and that kid, we're going to come to an understanding, Sage. I'm not crazy about this arrangement, neither are you, but we're going to have to deal. I'm not going anywhere. Start getting used to the idea."

Because he so badly wanted to frame her face with his hands, to lower his mouth to cover hers—God, it had been so long since he'd held her, tasted her, feasted on her—Tyce stood up and jammed his hands into the pockets of his jeans. Feeling wiped, he blew out a breath before locking eyes with Linc again. It was time to get this done.

"I've purchased enough shares to earn a seat on the Ballantyne board. I'm going to take that seat, I will oppose every decision and I will vote against every motion you make unless you actively try to establish whether Lachlyn is Connor's child or not. Do not underestimate how much trouble I can cause. I'll undermine your position and I'll actively campaign to have you removed as CEO."

Linc's face paled at the threat. But because he was a deal maker and a strategist, Linc then asked the question he was expecting. "So if Lachlyn is Connor's daughter, how much do you want?"

These rich people, they always thought it came

down to money. "I don't want any of your money," Tyce replied, enjoying the surprised shock on their faces. "If the DNA results come back saying that Lachlyn is not Connor's daughter, then I will sell the shares."

"What's the catch?" Beck demanded.

"If Lachlyn is Connor's daughter, then I'd like you to give her a chance…to get to know you, to become part of your family. She missed out on that, having a family."

So had he but that didn't matter. Lachlyn was the one who'd spent her childhood and teenage years in a dismal house permeated with the sadness of a perpetually depressed mother and a too tense, uncommunicative brother. She deserved the chance of being part of a close, happy family. And nobody, apparently, did family better than the Ballantynes.

Tyce held the back of a chair, his hands white against the black leather. He didn't drop his eyes from Linc's face, didn't break the contact. Linc, confusion all over his face, frowned. "I don't understand any of this. You spent tens of millions buying those shares but all you want is for us to give your sister a chance to get to know us?"

Tyce nodded. "You'll be happy to hear that she's a lot nicer than I am."

Linc's mouth twitched in what Tyce suspected might hint at amusement. He leaned back in his chair and folded his big arms across his chest. "This is bat-crap insane, Latimore."

"Probably," Tyce admitted, darting a look at the

still-fuming Sage. Oh, that reminded him. Hardening his expression, he looked from Linc's face to Jaeger's and then to Beckett's. "I have one more demand…"

Beck groaned and Jaeger swore. Linc just waited, his eyes narrowed.

"My last demand is that you leave us, Sage and me, alone. Having a baby, becoming new parents, is something new to both of us and we don't need her three angry, protective brothers muddying the waters."

God, he was tired of this conversation, so tired of it all. All he wanted to do was to climb into bed with Sage and wrap himself around her. He would even forego sex just to hold her and sleep.

Sage held up a hand and stopped what he was sure was going to be a hot response from Jaeger. Hot seemed to be Jaeger's default setting.

"You three don't need to fight my personal battles," Sage said, her voice clear and determined. "Tyce and I will deal with our personal situation, ourselves. Not—" Sage sent him a look that was designed to shrivel his balls "—that we have much to discuss."

"Are you sure, shrimp?" Jaeger asked her, doubt in his voice.

"Very." Sage nodded. "I can handle him."

"If he lays a finger on you, we will rip him from limb to limb and bury him so deep that no one will ever find his body," Beck added, his voice so flat and so bland that Tyce had no choice but to believe him.

"Tyce is an ass but he's not violent," Sage told them.

So nice to know how she really felt about him.

"Still…" Beck's eyes connected with his and Tyce nodded, acknowledging Beck's threat. Hurt her and he'd die. Got it.

"One tear, Latimore, and all bets are off," Linc said, rising to his feet. "We'll need a week or two, and your sister's DNA, to ascertain whether she is Connor's daughter and, if she is, we'll meet again, with your sister, to determine a path forward."

It was, Tyce realized, as much of a deal as he was going to get today and it was, honestly, better than he hoped. Lachlyn would finally have, if the Ballantynes cooperated, a shot at having the large, crazy, loving family she'd always said she wanted.

"Two weeks and then we'll reevaluate?" Tyce held out his hand and wondered if Linc would shake it. "Deal?"

Linc's warm hand gripped his and their gazes clashed and held. "Deal."

Linc dropped his hand, sidestepped him and opened the door to the conference room. "I'll contact you to set up the time and place for the DNA swabs." Linc walked out of the conference room and punched a code into the pad next to the elevator opposite the conference room. The doors slid open. Right, it was official; Linc was kicking him out.

Tyce ignored Linc's impatient expression and walked past Jaeger to drop to his haunches in front of Sage, resting his forearm across his knee. He waited until Sage lifted defiant eyes to meet his. "After you've spoken to your brothers, go home and sleep. I'm going to drop in this evening and—we'll talk then."

"I won't be there."

Tyce resisted the impulse to roll his eyes. "We need to talk, Sage. We can do it this afternoon or tomorrow morning but we are going to talk."

Sage muttered a curse under her breath and Tyce swallowed his smile at her hissed profanity. "Okay, this evening. Around five."

Tyce nodded, stood up and bent down again to drop a kiss on her head. Not wanting to see her reaction, her disgust, he spun around and headed out the door and into the lift. After punching the button for the ground floor, he looked at Sage and electricity, as it always did, hummed between them. He wanted to run back into the room, scoop her up and run away with her, to hell with Lachlyn and Sage's brothers. To hell with his art and her status as one of the wealthiest women in the world.

To hell with it all.

Unfortunately, Tyce thought as the elevator's doors closed, running away solved nothing.

The meeting had run longer than they thought and Beck and Jaeger left a few minutes after Tyce, both of them assuring her that they were in her corner, that they would help in any way they could.

"Up to and including beating the crap out of Latimore," Jaeger told her as a parting shot.

When she and Linc were alone Sage walked to the small window, laying her hand on the cool glass.

Droplets of icy rain ran down the pane and the low, gray clouds outside threatened snow. Late winter in New York City, she thought; she felt cold inside and out.

"You okay, shrimp?" Linc asked her. Sage turned, put her back to the wall and looked at her brother, his chair pushed back and his long legs stretched out.

"Mentally or physically?" Sage asked.

"Either. Both," Linc answered her.

Sage lifted one shoulder and shrugged, biting her bottom lip. Linc's eyes were on her face and she knew that her brother was hoping for an answer. Unlike Jaeger and Beck, Linc didn't nag and as a result, she found herself talking to him more often than anyone else.

Still, it was easier to stick to the facts. "I'm about twelve, thirteen weeks pregnant. I'm not seeing Tyce, it just happened."

Linc's expression was sober. "Do you want to keep this child?"

Now there was a question she could answer without hesitation. "With every breath I take."

Linc relaxed and his lightened. "Okay then. If you want to keep the baby, then we'll all pitch in to help you... You know that, right?" Linc stated.

Sage nodded. "I do. So does, apparently, Tyce." She tapped her index finger against her thigh. "I'm really surprised that he wants to be involved. I thought he'd take my offer to run."

Linc scowled. "A hell of a lot surprised me today and that was only one thing of many." Linc flipped through the folder Tyce had left and pulled out a letter-sized photograph of his sister, Lachlyn. He placed it on the table so that they could both look at the photo. "I can't deny that she looks like Connor, she has his eyes."

"And his nose," Sage added. Apart from their hair color, she and Lachlyn could almost be sisters.

Linc folded his arms. "He made quite a few threats today. Do you think he'd act on them?"

Sage knew he would. Tyce never said anything he didn't mean and she told her brother so. "The media is fascinated by him and, because he's so reclusive, when he speaks the world will sit up and listen."

"Crap."

"If his sister is Connor's daughter… God," Sage said, her voice trembling. She couldn't say more, hoping that her brother would know what she was trying to say without her having to verbalize her thoughts.

"If she's his daughter she's entitled to some part of his wealth? Is that what you are trying to say?" Linc asked her, pain in his eyes.

Sage nodded. "Isn't she? We're not his biological children, Linc. Yes, he adopted us but we're not his blood," Sage muttered. "If he knew about her, he would've scooped her up and pulled her into the family, his family."

"He wouldn't have tossed us aside," Linc stated, his voice full of conviction. "Connor had an enormous capacity for love."

"But he wouldn't have ignored her either."

Linc nodded, his face grave. "You're right. She would've been pulled into this family. And five people would've inherited his wealth and not four."

Sage traced the curve of Lachlyn's cheek with her finger.

Tyce's sister would've been hers, as well. The mind just boggled at the thought.

Linc rested his arms on the table, his brows lowered. "It's important that we take this one step at a time, that we don't get carried away. We need to do the DNA testing."

She had a sister; Connor had a child; there was a missing Ballantyne out there. Sage felt the world tilting and she leaned her back against the wall and closed her eyes. She couldn't do this; it was all too much. The pregnancy, Tyce, Lachlyn… Too much change.

And let's not forget the little detail of Tyce deliberately targeting her to gather information on her family. Their meet-cute at that art gallery had been anything but fortuitous. He'd intentionally set out to meet her with the goal of getting her to spill company information. And strangely, that hurt the most and made her doubt everything that had happened between them. Were they really that sexually compatible or had he been just pretending? Was he as attracted to her as she was to him? Had it all been one horrible, well-thought-out, excellent act on his part?

God, just the thought that the six weeks they'd spent together three years ago might be one-sided made her feel like someone was ripping out her internal organs without any pain relief.

Had he laughed at her, was he still laughing? Did he think she was a gullible idiot? That she was easily manipulated? God, she had to know.

Right now.

Sage lunged for her phone and pulled up his number, punching the green button. Tyce answered just after the first ring.

"Yeah?"

"Where are you?"

"In the alley behind the store—I went out the back exit," Tyce replied. "Why?"

"Wait there," Sage ordered, her skin prickling with embarrassment. She disconnected the call and picked up her coat, draping it over her arm. She could cope with a baby, with being on her own, but she didn't know how she would handle the truth that she was simply a means to an end for Tyce.

And a very easy lay.

God, she'd never felt more off-balance in her life. She looked at her favorite brother. "I'm going to go. I'll talk to you later."

Linc placed a hand on her shoulder and squeezed. "Shall we all have dinner at The Den tonight and you can break the news to the rest of the family? That way you can answer all the questions that I don't have the answers to."

Sage nodded. "Sounds good."

Linc pulled her into his arms and rubbed the top

of his chin across her head. When he spoke, his voice was rough with emotion. "Our baby is having a baby. How is that possible? How did it happen?"

Her eyes burning from unshed tears, Sage knew that in order to stop her tears from falling, she needed to diffuse the emotion swirling between them. "Well, Latimore and I met and then we stripped each other naked—"

Linc took a hasty step back and slapped his hands over his ears. "Shut up, shrimp. God, now I need brain bleach to get that picture out of my head."

Sage was a bundle of dread and anxiety.

She wanted to run away and hide, to do her ostrich impression—head in the sand—but at the same time she needed to know, she needed to have her worst fears confirmed.

Because when they were, she could, finally and without a smidgeon of doubt, bury those lingering doubts around whether walking away from Tyce three years ago was the right thing to do.

She'd know and she could be free of the what-ifs that occasionally plagued her. What if she was braver? What if she took a chance?

When he told her that it was all one-sided, then she could finally step away from him, physically and mentally.

At the door leading to the alley Sage punched the master code into the access panel and heard the click. She gave the heavy door a hard push and stumbled down the two steps that led into the narrow space behind the building.

"Easy there," Tyce said, grabbing her arms and keeping her from doing a face-plant.

Sage slapped his hands away and tossed him a scathing look. "Did you deliberately set out to meet me three years ago?"

Tyce frowned and his expression turned inscrutable. "Initially, yes."

"And after that?" Sage demanded, hearing the shrill note in her voice. "Did you keep sleeping with me to get information about the business and my family?"

"You didn't give any," Tyce pointed out.

"That's not the point! Did you use me for information?" Sage shouted, slapping her hands against his chest. "Did you keep sleeping with me because it was a means to an end? Were you into me, at all?"

Sage felt her ribs squeezing her heart and lungs and thought that her skin felt a size too small. She reminded herself to breathe, telling herself that she could deal with hearing that Tyce wasn't that into her, because it would give her the impetus she needed to stop thinking about him, dreaming about him, being tempted by him.

"Is that what you think?" Tyce asked, gripping her wrists and holding her hands against his broad chest. And, just like that, heat flowed into her and her fingers tingled with the need to touch and to explore. She could feel the slow, hard thump of her heart against her tight ribs and her nipples tightened, desperate for attention.

Tyce was touching her and that was all that was important...

"Are you seriously asking me whether I was pretending to be attracted to you?"

Tyce's harsh question reminded her that they were standing in an alley in the rain-tinged wind. Oh, and that she was as mad as hell with him.

"Are you insane?" Tyce demanded, his face saturated with frustration. He abruptly dropped her hands and slapped a hand on the top of her butt, jerking her into him. Sage released a surprised gasp when her stomach connected with the long, hard length of him. Holy cupcakes, he felt so good...

Tyce grabbed her elbows and lifted her off the ground, easily carrying her until her back touched the rough concrete wall. Holding both her wrists in one hand, he lifted her hands above her head, her breasts pushed into his chest. His deep, dark eyes met hers as he brushed her hair off her cheek. Sage held her breath as he slowly, so slowly dropped his head and his lips finally—God, he felt so good— covered hers.

His lips danced over hers, a soft, slow exploration, his tongue gentle as it wound around hers. She expected fire; she expected heat; she expected the maelstrom of want and need that always swirled between them but she didn't expect tenderness or reassurance. She didn't want to feel either. She wanted to be able to walk away from him, not be tempted to step closer… God, how could he make her feel like this?

Sage wrenched her mouth out from under his and glared up at him with what she hoped were stormy, accusing and not dreamy eyes.

"Did you kiss me to avoid the question?" she demanded, begging her heart to stop its relentless attempt to leave her chest. She dropped her eyes and, feeling the length of him still pressed against her, tried to pull her hands from his grip.

Tyce held her chin and forced her to look at him again. "I admit that I set out to meet you but this—" he hesitated "—crazy buzz between us had nothing to do with Lach-Ty, with the Ballantyne shares. It was, is, all you." He pushed his hard erection into her stomach and closed his eyes. "And me. You walk into the room and I immediately start thinking about how soon I can get you naked."

Dammit. His voice was deep and slow and lifted every hair on her neck. It made her want to feast on him, to gulp him up.

So much for finding some distance.

Tyce abruptly dropped her hands and stepped away from her, pushing his free hands into his hair. "It's cold and—" he nodded to the camera above their head "—not the most private place for either kissing or conversation. We'll talk more tonight."

Sage nodded, her head hurting with an overload of information and emotion.

Two thoughts ran through her head like toddlers on a sugar high: *I want him bad and it's so bad that I want him.*

Five

As an artist, Tyce immediately noticed the windows running from her floor to the ceiling, and massive skylights maximized the amount of light streaming into her loft apartment. This place was so Sage, he thought, looking around. The front door swiveled on a hinge in the middle of the frame as Sage closed the door behind him. The floor was comprised of light wooden planks holding a subtle tinge of pink. The wooden beams in the ceiling were partially stripped of their off-white cream paint, allowing the natural grain of the wood to bleed through. The entire loft was open-plan, except for a divider at the far end of the room, which suggested a bed and a bathroom hid behind. He looked up and saw the main bedroom overhead. There were two faded couches in a cream-and-nude stripe, beanbags tossed on the floor, and the back corner held her workbench and a massive corkboard containing sketches of her designs.

Tyce, because he appreciated the artist she was, immediately walked over to that wall, examining her sketches. There was an intricate diamond choker, a bracelet that reminded him of a serpent crawling up an arm and teardrop earrings. Tyce looked at her scribbled notes on each drawing where she'd detailed the stones she'd use. Four-carat emeralds here, a six-carat diamond there. Sage didn't play around.

Tyce lifted his finger up and tapped the letter-sized photograph of a ring sporting a massive red stone for its center and delicate diamond petals. Even he, stupid when it came to stones, could see that this was a serious piece of jewelry art.

"Is that a ruby?"

"It's a red diamond," Sage said, coming up to stand at his shoulder. "Ridiculously rare, practically flawless. It's—" she placed a hand on her heart and Tyce could see the emotion in her eyes "—the same chemical composition of coal but it amazes me that pressure and millions of years can turn coal into that."

"Is it really that red?" Tyce asked, intrigued.

Sage half smiled. "That photograph doesn't even begin to capture the color. It's a deep, luscious red that defies description."

"I take it that the Ballantyne family owns the ring?"

Sage nodded.

"Then why wasn't it with the rest of the collection at the cocktail-party-slash-exhibition? I thought the point of the exhibition was to display the fabulous stones your family has collected over the past hundred years. I'd say that this ring qualifies as fabulous."

Sage picked a pair of pliers, examined the handle and dropped them back onto the bench. "We decided not to show it to the world."

"Why not? Is it stolen?"

Sage glared at him. "No, it's not stolen." She sighed and Tyce noticed her eyes darkening with something akin to pain. "I asked Linc not to exhibit the ring. For personal reasons." Before he could ask what those personal reasons were Sage held up her hand and continued to speak. "Not going there, not now, not ever."

Yeah, good idea. Talking was a damn good way to crack the door allowing those pesky feelings to slide on through. They had enough to deal with as it was and they didn't need emotions muddying the water.

Bare feet peeking out from under the long hem of her jeans, Sage walked back to the center of the room and sat down on one of the two couches.

Tyce sat in the far corner on the couch opposite her, trying to put as much distance between them as possible. If she was in arms' reach, then there was a damn good chance that he'd say to hell with talking and take her to bed. As his lack of control in the alley earlier showed, resisting Sage was not something he'd ever excelled at. And, he admitted, making love to her would be like adding C-4 to a bonfire. Stupid and dumb-ass crazy.

They were adults and they had to have a mature conversation about their situation. Tyce thought that adulthood wasn't all that it was cracked up to be...

Then again, it was a damn sight better than being a child trying to operate in an adult world.

Sage pulled up her feet and tucked them beneath her bottom. She still looked a little shell-shocked and he couldn't blame her. Nothing was simple about this situation... Nothing ever would be.

While he wasn't a talker, he did concede that sometimes the only way to move forward was to communicate. Dammit, something else he wasn't great at.

"Are you still mad because I deliberately set out to meet you?" Tyce asked, keeping his voice mild.

"You used me!"

Initially he had. He'd asked her out that first night because she was Sage Ballantyne, because he'd just found out that Lachlyn was Connor's daughter and, in his anger, he'd thought that Sage was living Lachlyn's life. He'd expected to find a pampered princess, someone he would despise, but Sage had turned out to be totally different. She was funny, down-to-earth, a little crazy.

"Within an hour of meeting I established that, while you adored your family, you wouldn't talk about them. I also quickly realized that you weren't that interested in the business side of the company."

He caught the defiance in her eyes but he knew she was listening.

"If I was only interested in you for business information, I wouldn't have bothered to call you again," Tyce told her. "I paid a fair price for every share I purchased. I bought enough shares to bring Lachlyn to your attention, which was my eventual goal. Hearing that you are pregnant with my child moved my schedule up a bit. I haven't cheated anyone out of anything."

"You're blackmailing us!" Sage retorted but he saw the doubt in her expression. Tyce didn't feel offended, realizing that she was just trying to find solid ground, trying to make sense of this situation.

"I'm asking for DNA to be tested and if that DNA proves my theory, I am asking for my sister to meet you and your brothers. I am not asking for money, time or involvement." Tyce rested his forearms on his thighs, his eyes steady on her face.

Sage picked at the rip on her thigh, opening up a hole in the denim that wasn't there before.

She looked so lost and alone, out of her depth. Easily able to identify with those emotions, Tyce ignored his brain's insistence to play it cool. He moved across the bare wooden floorboards and dropped in front of her, bending his knees and linking his hands. "I wanted to tell you first, Sage, but you wouldn't take my calls."

Sage opened her mouth to argue and abruptly closed it again. Yeah, she couldn't argue that point. "You wouldn't talk to me so I went on to plan B."

Sage looked past him, to a painting on the far wall, and Tyce followed her gaze. It was the back view of a ballerina but unlike Degas's pretty, perfect renditions of the dancers, Tyce's piece was full of angst, accurately capturing the pain and persistence a dancer went through to achieve perfection. The dancer, dressed in a grubby tutu, her hair falling out of her bun, was massaging her toes, fatigue and pain radiating from her. It was one of his early pieces but emotion poured from it. It was good, he supposed. Not great, but good. Tyce idly wondered when Sage had bought it and why. He knew that she loved ballet but it wasn't, after all, a Degas, an artist whose work she could afford.

"Tell me about your sister," Sage commanded, her eyes clashing with his.

"What do you want to know and why?" Tyce asked, lifting an eyebrow at her imperious demand.

"Well, you want us to meet her. What does she do? What is she like?"

Tyce thought a moment, wondering what to say. He adored Lachlyn but he wasn't in the habit of talking about her. Or his family. "Uh…eight years younger than me. She's an archivist."

"Really? Does she enjoy her work?"

Tyce's mouth softened into a smile. "She loves it. She's history, and book, crazy."

Feeling antsy, Tyce rolled to his feet and walked across the room to look at the framed photographs on the wall. He smiled at a picture of a very young Sage in a tutu, attempting a pirouette, of Beckett on a diving board about to race, Jaeger and Linc in tuxedos at a wedding. All across the world were millions of walls like this one, holding ten billion memories.

He didn't have a wall, neither did Lachlyn.

Like most New Yorkers, he'd watched the Ballantynes grow up. The press was consistently captivated by the closest the city had to a royal family. He remembered the day their parents died, devouring the reports about their plane crash. Tyce remembered reading about Connor, a confirmed bachelor, stepping in and scooping up his orphaned nephews and niece. The Ballantynes had been, were, a constant source of fascination to the mere mortals of the city for a long time.

He had been amazed when Connor adopted Linc, his housekeeper's son, along with the three Ballantyne orphans. He'd wondered what type of man did that. Neither his own father, who'd bailed on him before he was old enough to remember him, or his stepfather ever gave a damn for anyone other than themselves. They'd both been so immature and unreliable, so it was no wonder that Connor's easy acceptance of children who weren't his made such an impression on him.

His mom just managed to keep it together enough to keep working, but navigating the world for a few hours a day sapped all her energy. She'd had nothing left to give to her son and her infant daughter. A month after he'd graduated from high school, his mom fell in on herself and refused to leave her room, to go back to work, to talk and to interact. Six weeks passed and Tyce knew that she wasn't getting better and that it was up to him to support his family. He gave up his scholarship to art school and found a job to feed, clothe and educate his ten-year-old sister. Since he worked two jobs and their mother slept as much and as often as possible, Lachlyn grew up alone. She'd craved a family, siblings, teasing, laughter and support but she got a mother who stopped speaking and a brother who retreated into an impenetrable cocoon, his thoughts consumed by how to stretch five dollars into ten, what new argument he could use to placate their landlord.

He and Sage couldn't be more different. They'd come from two situations that were polar opposites. She knew how to "do" family, to love and be loved in return. To support and be supported. He adored Lachlyn but love and support had fallen by the wayside when held up against his desire to keep them off the streets.

"What do you remember about Connor, about the time when he and your mom met?"

Tyce jammed his hands into the back pockets of his jeans. "As I said, my mom worked as a cleaner at Ballantyne International and I remember her leaving for work in the late afternoon and coming home as I got ready for school."

"Who looked after you?"

Tyce frowned at her. "What do you mean, who looked after me? I was seven, I looked after myself."

Sage's eyes widened. "She left you alone?"

"It wasn't like she had a choice, Sage," Tyce snapped back. "There wasn't money for a babysitter."

Sage laid a hand on her heart and looked horrified. God, they'd had such different childhoods. Sage probably hadn't been able to sneeze on her own at seven.

"Did she ever try to tell Connor about your sister?"

Tyce shook his head. "No. After she died, we found a letter she left for Lachlyn, telling her the truth. She said that she could see that she'd already reached the end of the road with Connor. She knew he was going to dump her."

"Connor didn't do long-term relationships," Sage said, her voice trembling. "It was just who he was... He felt trapped by people, by women. He never married or was engaged."

He could relate. He'd had the odd affair that lasted longer than a hookup but his relationships never lasted long because he always ended up feeling trapped. Funny, he'd never felt like that with Sage, possibly because they parted ways before he started to feel claustrophobic. But he had no doubt that it would've happened, that he would've eventually felt like he was running out of air.

Getting back to the subject... "When I heard that Lachlyn was Connor's daughter I tried to contact Connor but I couldn't get beyond his personal lawyers. They told me that many women have tried to scam Connor, saying that they had birthed his child. They told me to subpoena his DNA but I had no grounds to do that, especially since Lachlyn's birth certificate stated that my stepdad was her biological father. I couldn't prove jack."

"So you decided to buy Ballantyne shares." Sage bit her bottom lip, her eyebrows raised. "God, Tyce, that must have cost you a fortune."

Practically everything he had. "Yeah. But, at least, Lachlyn now owns a portion of what Connor created." Tyce rubbed the back of his neck. This was the longest conversation he'd had in a long, long time. But he still had more to say. "We both understand that Connor left his assets to his kids. He didn't know about Lachlyn and that's the card life dished out. I dished another card and she now owns shares in his company. That's enough for her, and me."

"Seriously?"

"Seriously," Tyce answered her, holding her eye. It was important that she realize he didn't want anything from her or her family. All he wanted was for Lachlyn to have a chance to meet them. Anything that happened after that was in the lap of the gods.

It was raining outside; he could hear the ping of droplets on her roof. Soft light bathed her apartment in pinks and cream and made Sage look younger and softer. They were alone; he could feel his heart pounding against his rib cage, heated blood pumping through his veins. The hair on the back of his neck and his arms stood up as all that warm blood headed south.

God, he wanted her. He always did, would… Tyce looked at her and clocked the exact time when her mind moved from Lachlyn to the attraction arcing between them. Her cheeks turned pink, her mouth softened and he could see her pulse beating in that delicate vee at the bottom of her throat. She stroked the arm of the couch, her fingers gliding over the fabric as they'd once glided over his erection. She had no idea that she'd subconsciously lifted her chest, that her nipples were pushing through the fabric of her bra and T-shirt.

One look and they were both jittery with need. He had to kiss her again, he couldn't resist...

Tyce moved across the floor quickly, stopping in front of her and placing his hands on the back of the sofa, on either side of her head.

Sage lifted her chin and shook her head. "Not happening, Latimore."

She didn't sound very convincing, Tyce thought. Besides he'd seen the flash of interest in her eyes, the smoky blues that suggested she was remembering how he made her feel. His junk immediately tightened and the hot, hard thump of his heart reminded him that it had been months since he'd had sex. Sage was the last woman he'd had in his bed and she was still, damn her, the only woman he wanted.

"I'd rather walk through cut glass without shoes than sleep with you," Sage defiantly muttered, dropping her eyes to stare at her hot-pink toes. Sexy toes with the middle toe sporting a delicate toe ring.

The saying about ladies and protesting too much dropped into his head but Tyce was smart enough not to verbalize that thought. He ran the back of his knuckles over her cheekbone and down the line of her jaw.

"You might not like me at the moment. You're angry and confused and feeling a bit overwhelmed by the fact you are pregnant and that my sister might be a Ballantyne but you still want me and I still want you."

Even though he knew it was a bad idea, Tyce leaned down. Their earlier kiss hadn't been nearly enough. He just needed to taste her again, once, maybe twice, and he'd be satisfied. He covered her mouth with his and sighed at the perfection of her silky lips. He swallowed a moan when those lips opened and his tongue slid into the hot, spicy space that was all Sage. He pulled her bottom lip between his teeth, nipped it and slid his tongue over the bite to soothe its sting. Sage's hand on the back of his neck held his head in place, her tongue dancing with his as her other hand pulled his shirt up to find his bare skin.

He had to stop this now, but he couldn't, didn't want to. He wasn't satisfied; he wanted more. When it came to Sage he always wanted more: one kiss, one bout of sex, was never enough. She was like the most addictive drug in the world. He doubted that there would ever be a time when he wouldn't want Sage Ballantyne and that complicated the hell out of this situation. He had to stop…

Tyce pulled away, lifted his mouth from hers and leaned backward, raising his hands in the air. Sage's mesmerizing eyes slowly refocused and when she was fully in the present, she shook her head and let out a whimper. "What the hell is wrong with us?" she whispered.

"An inability to talk, a desire to avoid anything that smacks of intimacy combined with white-hot heat," Tyce retorted, pushing his hands through his hair. He stood up, willed his junk to subside and walked over to the large windows, staring out at the wet street below him. Night was falling and he and Sage hadn't progressed one inch.

"We need a new way of dealing with each other," he muttered, jamming his hands into the pockets of his jeans. In the reflection of the glass he could see her pulling her long hair off her face, raising her knees to her chest and wrapping her arms around her legs. "I'd say that we should try to be friends but that's ridiculous, since we both know that friends don't generally want to rip each other's clothes off."

"I'm not very good at being a friend."

Tyce, intrigued by that odd statement, turned around to look at her. "What do you mean by that?"

Sage made a production of looking at her watch. She gasped, wrinkled her nose and jumped to her feet. "I'm so late! I have to go to The Den and break the news that I am pregnant to Jo—"

"Jo?"

"Linc's mom. Connor employed her as a housekeeper when he adopted us and she became our second mom. And my brother's wives are going to be pissed that my siblings heard the news first."

Tyce lifted his eyebrows. "You avoided my question."

Sage handed him a snotty look but her eyes begged him not to pursue the topic. "I really do need to get to The Den and I really am late," she said, walking to the door.

And you really don't want to explain why you think that you are a bad friend. Tyce walked across the room to pick up his leather jacket and scarf. Making a quick decision, based purely on the fact that he wasn't ready to walk away from Sage just yet— something he'd worry about later—he tossed the suggestion out. "What if I go with you and help you drop the news?"

Sage, holding her shoe, stared at him with panic-filled eyes. "You can't! They aren't ready for you, for us… I need to tell them on my own."

Tyce shook his head. "The sooner they get used to the idea that I am going to be hanging around, the easier this situation will become." And really, irritating her brothers would be an added bonus.

"Tyce…" Sage's eyes slammed into his. "Please, I need some time. Your revelations today, the pregnancy, my family… You've known about your sister for years and…we've only just learned about her. We need time to catch up, to process all of this."

Tyce considered her statement, impatience and a need to move forward warring with her words. She did have a point, he reluctantly conceded. They were playing catch-up and he needed to give her, and her family, time to do that.

Tyce opened her front door and held it open. "Okay, I hear you. But we still have more to discuss, a lot more."

"I know…we didn't get very far tonight," Sage said, pulling on a long navy coat and winding a cashmere scarf around her neck. "But I need some time, Tyce, and some space. I'll call you."

He wanted to argue, to have a firm date and time in mind but he also knew that, if he pushed her, she'd retreat back inside her shell. It was, after all, exactly what he would do.

"You'd better. And soon," Tyce told her, bending to drop a kiss on her temple. He stepped away and touched her stomach with the tips of his fingers. His kid, growing inside her. God, what a concept. "Take care of yourself, Sage. Call me if you need me."

Sage sent him a puzzled look, her expression stating that she couldn't imagine a situation in which she might need him. She had three brothers, three new sisters and more money than God. She didn't need him for anything except, possibly, sex and that wasn't on the table. Tyce ran his hand through his hair and followed her into the elevator opposite her front door.

He looked at their reflection in the mirror finish of the lift. Sage's hands were in her hair—where his really wanted to be—and twenty seconds later she'd, somehow, secured all those waves into a messy knot at the back of her neck. She pulled a tube of lipstick from the side pocket of her bag and swiped the color across her lips, turning her mouth from sweet to luscious. The lipstick was returned to the bag and a multicolored scarf appeared in her hand. She twisted it around her neck, tied it into a complicated knot and she was, once again, Sage Ballantyne, heiress, ready to face the world.

Tyce glanced at his outfit, old jeans, hiking boots, a black sweater over a black shirt and a leather bomber jacket that he'd had for too many years to count. Sage was an heiress from a family whose blood ran blue; he was an artist who genuinely thought that the art world would one day wake up from their stupor and realize that he wasn't half as good as they'd proclaimed him to be and definitely not worth the ridiculous money the collectors paid for his work. He plowed the bulk of the money he earned from his art into buying those Ballantyne International shares so he was, well, not broke but he wasn't flush with cash either. He didn't have a college degree and his only asset was a battered warehouse on the edge of an industrial park.

He was her former lover, the father of her child… the man who'd given her the bare bones of a very complicated story involving both their families, too scared to open up and make even the smallest emotional connection. He was also the man who wanted her more than he wanted to keep breathing, existing. His raging need to strip her naked and sink inside was part of the problem, he reluctantly admitted, but it went deeper than that.

Sage was, had always been, in a class of her own. She was funny and smart and generous and, surprisingly, she was the most down-to-earth girl he knew.

She had no idea that her smile could stop traffic, that her legs could make grown men weep, that her eyes could be weaponized. She had the ability to cut him off at the knees and that was the primary reason why he needed to keep her at a distance. He could fall into something deeper with Sage. She was the one woman who could tempt him into opening up, to explore a world that went beyond some bed-based fun.

Tyce banged the back of his head on the wall of the elevator, feeling his throat constrict. His mind was all over the place, as unsettled as a raging river. She'd always had the ability to mess with his thoughts, to disturb his equilibrium.

He'd explained about the shares, about Lachlyn, and it would be at least two weeks until the DNA tests came back. Sage said that she needed space and, yeah, judging by his crawling skin and accelerated breathing, maybe he did too. He'd take some time, put some distance between them, get his head on straight, to figure out how to deal with Sage on a long-term basis.

A basis that didn't, sadly, involve getting her naked.

Six

Sage glanced at her laptop screen and frowned at the brief message from Linc that had popped into her inbox five minutes ago.

DNA testing confirms that Lachlyn Latimore is Connor's biological daughter. Family meeting?

Family meeting? What did that mean anymore? Did that mean just her and her brothers, her brothers plus their partners, Lachlyn, Tyce?

They were all now connected through DNA. She was connected to Lachlyn because their fathers were brothers, she was connected to Tyce through the DNA their baby shared. It was all crazy, too much to handle. She had a cousin. A sister, sort of. Who was also her baby's aunt.

The news that Lachlyn was Connor's daughter wasn't a surprise: from the moment she saw Lachlyn's photo she'd known who'd fathered her. How to interact with Lachlyn, what to do, how to approach her had played on an endless loop in her head over the past ten days. They were frequently joined by *How involved does Tyce want to be with the baby?* and *What would he do if I jumped him?*

The question of Tyce's role as a father was constructive thinking; the thoughts and memories of Tyce's muscled body and his skilled mouth, and rediscovering what lay under his clothes, were not.

Throwing her pencil onto her workbench, she picked up the sketch she'd been working on—resetting an eight-carat cabochon-cut diamond—scrunched it into a ball and tossed the piece of paper over her shoulder. Her concentration was shot; she couldn't draw a stick figure if someone put a gun to her head.

Sage pushed her chair back and walked across her loft to the windows to look at her city. Linc's email sealed the deal—Lachlyn was Connor's daughter and was a Ballantyne. That meant changes and Sage wasn't fond of change. In her experience change meant sadness and grief. Every time change slapped her it hurt like hell: her parent's deaths, Connor's death. Change always meant tears and she was quite convinced she'd shed enough of those.

Lachlyn's connection to her family meant that Sage had to make an effort to know her, to pull her into the family circle. It was such a big ask. God, she was still getting used to her siblings' women and she was still finding her way with them. She adored Piper, Cady and Tate but she didn't understand them. How could they be so open, so unafraid? They lived bold lives, believing, erroneously in her opinion, that their lives would only and forever be wonderful. Her parents had lived like that: fearlessly, daringly, without worrying about the future, without worrying that life could smack them in a hundred and ten different ways. She'd experienced that intense grief when her parents died, again with Connor's death.

Nobody understood that fear kept her sane, that standing apart from people gave her some measure of control, a tiny barrier to deflect the hard wallop of people dying, leaving, moving away...*changing*.

Sage heard the first bars of her ringtone and looked at the screen of her phone and hesitated. She should answer Tyce's call but fear and frustration kept her hands firmly in the pockets of her jeans. She ran her hands over her face as a wave of guilt crashed over her. She'd promised to call him but she was still digesting him and their situation, desperately hoping that her fairy godmother would creep into her loft and wave a wand and make sense of her life. It would be easier if she knew what she wanted from Tyce, how she wanted to raise this child, how to start a conversation with him.

The problem was that every time she laid eyes on him, her brain shut down and her body started to thrum. Desire coursed through her and skin prickled and her stomach quivered. She wanted to make love to him again, to explore the angles and ridges of his muscled body and hear him moan with need for her. She imagined his fingers on her, in her, his mouth licking its way down her body, testing her, tasting her, filling her…

Sage placed the palm of her hand against her forehead. Tyce was an alpha male, possibly the most alpha male she'd ever met. He was ridiculously fit and almost overwhelmingly male and thoughts of him made her womb throb and her lady parts tingle.

Okay, this was ridiculous; she was burning up from the inside out. There had to be an explanation for why she was feeling a hundred times hornier than usual…

Tyce was ludicrously good-looking and phenomenally talented at getting her off, but even when she was younger, she'd never felt so on edge, so aware of her libido. Usually when she was stressed—and the events of the past few weeks were enough to stress out a sloth—her libido took a dive.

Her horniness could be pregnancy hormones, she decided and, almost immediately, cursed herself for lying to herself. It was all Tyce, only Tyce. God, maybe she needed a cold shower.

Sage looked out her windows at the dingy day. Or maybe a walk in fresh air would do the trick. Although it was snowing, a brisk walk would clear her mind and work out some of the tension in her body. Making up her mind, Sage headed to her front door, pulling on flat, warm boots and a thick coat. She

placed a floppy burgundy hat over her messy hair
and wound a scarf around her neck. Her gloves were
in her pocket and with her front door key, her phone
and a little cash, she headed downstairs.

It was colder than she'd thought. Sinking her chin
into her scarf, she pulled on her gloves and started to
walk. In summer the trees were leafy and the cafés
scattered chairs and tables on the sidewalk but on a
bitter winter afternoon, with snow falling, the resi-
dents of this neighborhood were either in Florida, at
work or tucked up in their apartments. Only fools
and the insane walked the streets in a biting wind.
She wouldn't last long, Sage thought; she'd walk a
block or two to clear her head and when she returned
to her apartment she could justify a decadent cup of
hot chocolate. Damn, it was slippery, she thought
when her feet skidded across a patch of ice. Maybe
this wasn't such a great idea.

Turning back to her apartment building, Sage saw
a tall figure approach her front door and frowned,
thinking that his height and build reminded her of
Tyce. When he walked up the steps and jabbed his
finger on her button she recognized his profile, the
odd snowflake settling on his black hair. Tyce was
leaning on her bell, waiting for her to buzz him in.
Impatient man, Sage thought, stepping from the road
onto the sidewalk.

Because her eyes were on Tyce, she didn't notice the patch of ice and her right foot skidded out
from under her. Her left foot followed suit and then
she was freewheeling her arms, trying to keep her

balance. Can't fall, she thought, she had to protect her baby. She tried to break her fall and her hand slammed down on the pavement and she heard the distinctive crack.

The pain in her coccyx hit her first, the sharp sting rocketing up her spine. Not wanting to be out-done, her wrist radiated short, sharp bursts of agony, causing dots to appear behind her eyes and her breath to catch in her throat.

Sage knew she didn't call out to Tyce—she had no breath to speak let alone to yell—but by some miracle he appeared and dropped to his knees next to her. "Crap! Sage, are you okay? What the hell happened?"

Sage, still looking for air and fighting pain, couldn't reply.

Tyce's hand on her cheek anchored her and his deep, calm voice steadied her. "Okay, honey, just breathe. Slowly. In and out."

Sage concentrated on getting air into her lungs, vaguely aware that Tyce held a phone to his ear, his eyes locked on hers. She heard something about an ambulance, that they should hurry. Sage tried to wave his concerns away; she would be okay; she just needed a minute.

And, she thought, a new coccyx and a new wrist. Then she would be fine.

"Yeah and she's pregnant, about four months," Tyce said. "Breathe, dammit."

Okay, that statement was directed at her. Sage pulled in some more air and felt the light-headedness pass and the pain increase. She was also, she realized, lying flat on her back and every inch of her body was freezing, except for her butt and her wrist, both of which were on fire.

Tyce pushed his phone back into the inside pocket of his jacket and pushed a strand of hair out of her eyes.

"I need to sit up," Sage rasped. "I'm cold."

"They said not to move you," Tyce replied, his hand covering her stomach.

"I'm freezing, Tyce." Sage heard the distant wail of ambulance sirens and wrinkled her nose. "That for me?"

Tyce looked up and nodded. "Yep."

"I'm sure that's not necessary."

"What wasn't necessary was you going out on a freezing day and endangering yourself," Tyce growled as the ambulance pulled up beside them.

"I needed air," Sage protested.

"Then open a damned window!" he retorted as EMTs approached them.

"We're going to need you to stand back, sir."

Tyce stood at the young female EMT's command and Sage noticed that his jeans were soaked from the knees down. That meant, she supposed, that she was wet from tip to toe. Wet and cold. "Any cramping? Any signs that you might be bleeding?" the EMT asked her as he pointed a penlight at her eyes.

"Nope," Sage replied. "I bounced off my butt. Look, my apartment is right over there—if someone can help me up, then I'll go on upstairs and I'll be fine."

The EMT looked up and Sage saw him exchange a look with Tyce. "I strongly suggest that, because you are pregnant and because you are cradling your hand like a baby, you go to hospital." Sage nodded, sighed and looked at her front door, so near but so far away. She really, really needed that cup of hot chocolate.

"They x-rayed my wrist and I have a greenstick fracture, which is why I have this stupid cast."

"Are you allowed to have X-rays when you're pregnant?"

Tyce heard Linc's question and quickly realized that Sage was talking to her brother via speakerphone and waited to hear her answer. Stopping, he stood to the side of the partially open door to her hospital room and put his back to the wall, holding a small bag containing dry clothes and shoes. Luckily the hospital wasn't far from her apartment and Sage had handed over the key so that he could collect clothes for her to wear home.

"I checked—they said it was completely safe," Sage said, sounding bone-deep weary. Tyce ran a hand over his eyes, the image of her feet flipping up and her butt hitting the pavement with a loud thump playing over and over in his head. Okay, she hadn't been knocked by a car but she'd landed hard and he kept expecting to see blood soaking through her jeans.

Tyce felt his stomach lurch into his throat at the

thought. Up until a few hours ago he'd understood Sage's pregnancy on a purely intellectual basis: his sperm, her egg, a baby later in the year. But when she fell, he felt bombarded with fear. How badly was she hurt? How could he fix her? What could he do? What if she lost this baby? How would she feel?

How would *he* feel?

Lousy, he decided. Sage's baby, he realized, their baby, wasn't something he wanted to wish away.

When had that happened? And how?

"Are you sure you don't want me to come down? I can be there in about a half hour," Linc said.

Tyce held his breath, waiting for her answer.

"I'm sure Tyce will see me home. He was with me when I fell."

"Then he did a piss-poor job of catching you," Linc grumbled.

"He was at my door and I was stepping onto the pavement. He's not Superman, Linc."

Silence fell between the siblings and Tyce straightened, prepared to enter the room again. He stopped when Linc spoke again. "If your right wrist is in a cast and if walking causes you pain, then you can't stay on your own."

Linc was right, Tyce thought. Sage needed help for a while and maybe he should be the one to offer to stay with her. Sure, living with her and not making love to her was going to be hellfire difficult but the reality was that they couldn't keep circling round each other. At some point they had to start dealing with each other. And it would be better for the baby if they managed to establish some sort of a relationship—hopefully something that resembled a friendship—before their child dropped into the world and their lives.

Tyce fully accepted that he was a loner, that he didn't need people but he was connected to his child and through that little person to Sage. He doubted he could give the child what he or she needed but, along with offering whatever financial support he could to Sage, he was prepared to try to be a dad. That way, he could look himself in the eye and say that he'd tried to be the best father he could. Part of this new role was looking after his child's mother. And if that meant moving in with her and helping out while she was injured, that was what he intended to do.

Seven

"Let me talk to the brothers and we'll draw up a roster so that one of us will stay with you until you can manage on your own," Linc replied.

"I'm not a hundred and three, Linc! I don't need anyone to stay with me. You know I hate having people in my space."

Tough, Tyce thought, despite the little spurt of sympathy he felt for her. He didn't like people in his space either but she'd just have to suck it up and deal.

"I'll stay with you tonight—"

That was his cue, Tyce thought. Nobody was staying with her but him. He walked into the room, dumped her clothes on the foot of her bed and walked around the bed to look down at Sage's phone into

Linc's worried face. Taking it from her hand, he ignored Sage's annoyed "Hey!"

"Forget the roster, Linc. I'll be staying with her."

"Latimore," Linc said, his eyes and tone cool. "Is that what Sage wants?"

Judging by her annoyed and fractious expression, Sage would rather have a mutant cockroach move in but he didn't care. He was looking after Sage so that she could look after their baby.

And maybe you're also doing this because you need to know that she is okay on a day-by-day, minute-by-minute basis? Tyce ignored the errant thought. He looked at Sage, who was squawking her displeasure.

"Pipe down, Sage. It's a done deal, Linc," Tyce said before disconnecting the call.

Her eyes hazy with pain, Sage tried to skewer him with a look. "You are not coming home with me and you are not moving in!"

Tyce jammed his hands into the back pockets of his jeans, conscious that the bottom half of his jeans was still damp from kneeling on the sidewalk beside her. He opened his mouth to argue with her and then noticed her pale face and pain-filled eyes. Dammit, he hated knowing that she was in pain and that there was nothing he could do about it.

Arguing with her was a waste of energy: he was taking her home and he was temporarily, very temporarily, moving in. As he'd told Linc, it was a done deal.

Placing both hands on the bed on either side of

her hips, he looked into her face. "No BS. How, exactly, are you feeling?"

Sage opened her mouth, shut it again and the heat of her sigh caressed his chin. "The baby is fine. I'm not at risk of miscarrying if that's what you are worried about," she said in a quiet voice.

She had no idea that he wasn't half as concerned about the baby as he was about her. The baby had its own custom-made airbag; Sage hadn't had anything between her and the cold, hard sidewalk.

"Sage..." Tyce used his knuckle to lift her face up, waiting until their eyes connected again before he spoke. "I know that but I want to know how *you* are feeling."

"My wrist is sore but bearable, but my tailbone is excruciating. It hurts to sit."

Tyce had to touch her so he cupped the side of her face. "Have you had some pain meds?"

"Just acetaminophen. They also gave me some cream to help with the bruising." She looked at her wrist, closed her eyes and sighed. "That's not something I'm going to able to manage myself."

Tyce laid his lips on her forehead, holding the kiss there for longer than necessary. *She's okay*, he reminded himself as panic clawed up his throat. *She's okay...and the baby is okay... Breathe.* When the unfamiliar wave of, God, *emotion* passed—yeah, Sage's superpower was to turn him to mush—Tyce pulled back and dragged a smile onto his face. "I happen to like your butt and I have no problem touching it, with cream and without."

As he hoped, Sage rolled her eyes and amusement touched her lips. She picked up her phone from the side table and sent Tyce an uncertain look. "Are you sure you want to look after me for a couple of days? Wouldn't it be easier if my family took turns to help me out?"

Tyce straightened. "Probably. The thing is, Sage, you and I need some time to talk, to get to know each other again. We didn't spend that much time talking three years ago."

She blushed and Tyce knew that she was remembering the hours, days they spent in bed…not talking. "In less than half a year," he added, "we'll have this child and it will be affected by everything we do, from how we talk to each other, treat each other, interact with each other. I genuinely believe that we have to try to find a sensible way of dealing with each other."

"And you think that way is to move in with me and rub cream on my butt?" Sage asked, skeptical.

"If I move in for a few days, we'll have time to talk, to figure out a way forward, to talk about this baby and how it will change our lives. We can discuss your expectations, my expectations, how we're going to tackle this." Tyce pushed his hands into his hair, frustrated. The adults in his life had lurched from crisis to crisis, had been reactive rather than proactive. By moving in with her, she couldn't avoid him and he'd be able to find out what type of father Sage wanted him to be and whether he could live up to her expectations.

They could build something small but meaningful between them, some type of relationship that would help them to co-parent their child effectively. Yeah, it meant him stepping out of his comfort zone, opening up a little, but his child deserved his best effort. Tyce sucked in a deep breath. They needed a plan and with one in place, there was less chance they'd go off script and venture into unknown, scary, emotional territory. "Am I making any sense?"

Sage wrinkled her nose. "Unfortunately, yes."

"Your enthusiasm is underwhelming," Tyce stated, his voice dry.

Sage tried to swing her legs off the bed and groaned. She closed her eyes and Tyce's heart contracted at her low whimper. "Dammit, that hurts."

Thinking that the easiest way to get her onto her feet was to lift her, Tyce slid one arm around her back, the other under her knees, and easily lifted her into his arms. Backing away from the bed, he looked down into her lovely face. "Okay?"

"Yeah." Sage curled her hand around his neck and lust skittered down his spine. "I'm okay. You can put me down."

"I'll keep my hands on you so that you don't fall," Tyce told her, keeping his voice steady and calm. After Sage was on her feet, he held her elbows and checked her face for pain. Seeing that she was coping, he leaned back and snagged the bag of clothes from the bed. He'd wanted, desperately, to remove her clothes but not like this. He'd intended to kiss every inch of her skin as he undressed her, inhale her scent, drive her crazy.

Sage's eyes slammed into his and, despite her pain, he saw the flash of awareness, heard her quick intake of breath. He couldn't help noticing that the gap between her thighs widened, that she'd subconsciously arched her back, a silent signal that desire bubbled under her pain.

He had to be the better person here... Sage was injured and he was sex deprived. But it would help if she stopped looking at him like he was a piece of fine Belgian chocolate that she couldn't wait to sample.

"Stop looking at me like that," he grumbled.

"Like what?" Sage asked, her face flushing.

"Like you want me to get you naked," Tyce snapped. "You're injured and I need to get some dry clothes on you. I shouldn't be thinking about how it feels to hold you naked, up close and against me."

Sage pulled her plump bottom lip between her teeth. "Are we ever going to get past this, Tyce?"

"Me wanting you?" Tyce clarified.

"And me wanting you." Sage rubbed her eye socket with the ball of her hand. "We keep telling ourselves that we can ignore this heat between us but it's constantly there, like the proverbial elephant in the room."

Nailed it, Tyce thought. Forcing his big brain to think, he pulled out her clothes from the bag. "We have so much else to deal with that I think we should keep our lives as simple as possible. Sex always adds a layer of complication."

"I suppose you're right."

He was but this was one time when he didn't want to be. He wanted to have her, take her and damn the consequences, but he knew that those complications would come back and take a solid chunk out of his emotional ass.

Be smart, Latimore.

"Okay then. If you have a car waiting, let's not worry about my clothes. I can handle the cold for a few minutes," Sage told him, cradling her plaster-cast arm.

"Probably, but you'd be a lot more comfortable, and warmer, in yoga pants and a hoodie than in those scratchy scrubs the nurse found for you to wear."

"I refused a hospital gown."

Tyce gestured to the sterile, unattractive hospital room. There was less chance of them getting carried away here than there was at her apartment.

"Let's just get this done."

Pulling out her clothes from the bag, Tyce stopped to look at her. Her cheekbones were slightly red. They'd discussed this, discussed making love, why was she now embarrassed? Girls could be so weird about their bodies and nudity. "Honey, I have kissed, tasted and explored every inch of you. What's the problem with me seeing you in your bra and panties?"

Sage's shoulders lifted up to hover around her ears. "That was sex. This is…I don't know how to explain it…this is different."

It was more intimate, Tyce realized. And intimacy

scared Sage, as it did him. She liked being in control of what she shared with him and how much of herself she gave him and she was suddenly thrust into a situation where she had to allow him control. Tyce sympathized. He didn't like losing control either. He dropped a hand onto her shoulder and squeezed before holding up a pair of soft, well-worn yoga pants.

"So, those clothes or these?" he asked in his most businesslike voice.

Sage nodded at her pants. "Those, please." She started to fiddle with the band of her scrub pants with her left hand, muttering soft curses. "God, it even hurts to stand."

Tyce dropped to his haunches, whipped her pants down and off, trying to ignore those long, gorgeous legs that had wrapped around his hips, back and neck many times in the past. Ignoring the wave of memories, he slid the yoga pants over her lifted foot and then the other. *Just get it done, Latimore.* He pulled the stretchy fabric up her legs, standing up to pull the material over her butt. He glanced down and noticed the football-size bruise starting to form on her lower back. "Holy hell, Sage, how hard did you fall?"

"What?"

"You have a hell of a bruise on your butt. That's why sitting hurts," Tyce said, reaching for her socks. He quickly put her sneakers on her feet and tied the laces. Standing, he lifted the top half of her scrubs up her torso and gently pulled the shirt over her arm, trying to keep his eyes off her round, firm breasts half covered by a dusky-pink lacy bra that matched the color of her thong. God give him strength! And please, God, make her injuries heal fast; he couldn't wait to have her under him again... No, wait, that wasn't on the agenda; that wasn't part of the plan. The mission was to find a new way of dealing with each other and not to reexplore the missionary position.

Sex, moron, he chided himself, *will only add a truckload of complicated to an already convoluted situation. Did you not say that ten minutes ago?*

"Are you okay?" Sage asked him as he dropped a long-sleeved T-shirt over her head.

"Not even close," Tyce muttered under his breath. He picked up her hoodie, threaded her injured arm through the sleeve and frowned at the blank canvas of her plaster cast. "I'm going to have to make that more gangsta."

"Huh?"

Tyce tapped her cast. "It's white and boring. We'll graffiti it up."

The corners of her mouth tipped up. "It'll be the most expensive cast in the history of the world. You'd better sign it so that when it's removed someone can sell it on the net and make a fortune."

Tyce finished dressing Sage, helped her with her sling and picked up the spare coat he'd brought with him. "Right, let's bust you out of here."

Sage took one step, yelped, took another and groaned. Not bothering to ask her, he picked her up and held her against his chest, his temple against her head. "Better?"

"Much," Sage murmured as her good arm encircled his neck. "Though they are going to insist on a wheelchair, hospital policy."

"They can insist until the air turns blue, I'm not letting you go," Tyce told her, walking in the hallway.

I'm not letting you go.

Why did that statement resonate with him? Tyce couldn't understand why that particular order of words made deep, fundamental sense. This was the problem with being around Sage, he thought, and the reason why he'd backed away all those years ago. With her, strange thoughts and concepts popped into his head.

Keeping her, he fiercely, and silently, told himself, wasn't an option, not then and not now. He liked his own company, liked the freedom of not being tied down to a woman, a place, city or town. If he wanted to he could leave New York and go to Delhi or Djibouti; he could go anywhere. Lachlyn would be fine. He would sell or rent his space and he could take off. He could only do that because he was free of commitments; he didn't have another person to consider, someone else's feelings and wishes to take into account.

He wouldn't have to explain…

Maybe when Sage was back to full strength, he'd backpack for a couple of months. He could travel, only coming home a week or two before the baby was due to be born.

But then, he thought as he lowered Sage into the back seat of the waiting taxi, he'd miss seeing Sage's tummy grow with life, would miss the ultrasound scans, the doctor's visits. Could he do that? Could he leave?

He so badly wanted to say yes, to be convinced that she would be fine, but uncertainty twisted his stomach, his gut instinct insisting that he wasn't going anywhere, that he was going to see this process through.

So no Delhi or Djibouti then. That was okay, Tyce thought as he took the seat next to Sage. He could deal.

Much later that afternoon Sage's eyes fluttered open and she pulled in the familiar scent of her apartment… She was home, in a bed. Rolling over, she yelped. Every inch of her body was sore, from the back of her head to her shoulders, her damned tailbone, her legs. Her wrist throbbed. Glancing down at her cast, she sucked in an astonished gasp. Her plaster cast was no longer white but filled with miniature portraits, all wickedly accurate. Linc, Jaeger, Beck, Jo, Connor—God, Connor's picture looked so like him, his patrician face wearing a huge smile. Tyce had sketched her nephews, her niece. Her brother's partners. She could see that they'd been drawn quickly but, quick or not, they were fantastic. It was another reminder that Tyce was phenomenally talented…

"I was bored."

Sage's eyes shot up to see Tyce leaning against the half wall that separated the spare bedroom from the rest of the apartment. Uncomfortable with Tyce carrying her up the narrow staircase to her bedroom, she'd told him she'd be fine in the spare.

She immediately noticed the smudges of charcoal on his white T-shirt and faded jeans. Sage traced the outline of Connor's face with her finger, happy to see that the lines didn't blur. "They are fantastic. How did you seal them to stop them from smudging?"

"There was a tin of clear lacquer under your workbench." Tyce shrugged. "Thanks to your obsession with framing photographs, I managed to get them all."

"They are amazing. How long did they take you to do?"

Tyce shrugged. "Not long. I would've been quicker but you kept distracting me."

She distracted him? How on earth? "I was asleep when you did this!" she protested.

"You've always been beautiful but I'd never watched you sleep before. You're simply stunning," Tyce said, sounding utterly sincere.

Sexual awareness arced between them and Sage pushed her fingers into her hair, thinking that it felt odd to wake up with someone in her home. She felt a little self-conscious, a tiny bit awkward but, mostly, having Tyce in her apartment made her feel protected, cared for. Safe.

Safe? Not possible, Sage thought. She hadn't felt safe for years, not truly safe, not since before her parents were alive. She was misreading what she was feeling; she had to be because safe wasn't something she expected to feel, would allow herself to feel, ever again.

Either way, it was time she stopped.

Sage rolled onto her back and winced, using her good arm to push up. In a flash Tyce was at her side, strong arms helping her up the bed so that she could lean against her headboard. He disappeared into the bathroom and came back with a glass of water and two pills. "Acetaminophen—they'll take the edge off."

"Thanks." Sage took the pills, threw them into her mouth and chased them down with a long pull of water. Right, it was time to take back control. She needed her home back, some distance between her and whatever she was feeling for Tyce.

"I appreciate you bringing me home from the hospital, for watching out for me, but it's time for you to go."

Tyce just lifted one dark eyebrow in response. "No."

Sage glared at him. This was her apartment; he was here only because she allowed it. "Tyce, I don't like having people in my space, in my face."

"I don't either but—" Tyce shrugged "—tough." He pointed at her stomach. "In less than six months we're both going to have a new person in our lives— a very demanding creature if I understand the process correctly. So maybe we should try to, and get used to, the notion of sharing space so that we don't die from shock."

Sage's mouth dropped open. What was happening? She was trying to push him away but he wasn't budging. This wasn't how this was supposed to go! When she pushed people away, most people were polite enough to give her the distance she needed.

Not Tyce.

Then again, she was quite convinced that God broke the mold after Tyce was born. One of him, she was pretty sure, was all the world, and she, could handle.

What could she say to make him leave?

"I'm going to be around for a few days so…you might as well get used to it."

Crap.

Tyce continued speaking, utterly at ease. "So, while you were sleeping, I answered what felt like a million calls from your family." Tyce took her empty glass and placed it on the bedside table. He sat down on the side of the bed, lifting his knee up onto her comforter, and resting his hand on the far side of her leg. His other hand gripped her thigh. "I don't normally talk to that many people in a month, let alone in an afternoon."

She was trying to keep up with the conversation, she really was, but his hand on her leg turned her brain to mush.

Sage could feel the size and shape, the heat of it through the covers and her yoga pants. If his hand moved a little up, and a little in, he'd find her happy spot—

Aargh! Really?

Sage mentally gave herself a head punch and

pulled her focus back to their conversation. "Well, that doesn't surprise me. You were never chatty."

"Oh, I can mingle and make small talk when I need to, although it's very dependent on whether I want to. I don't often want, or need, to."

"And, let's face it, people like your surly and brooding attitude. It's, apparently, sexy," Sage muttered.

"Only apparently?" Tyce murmured, leaning forward, his eyes on her mouth. Sage's breath caught and held as he moved closer and her heart rate inched upward. He hovered just above her, prolonging the anticipation, and then his mouth met hers in a kiss as seductive as it was sweet. There was passion in his kiss, but it was banked, restrained. This kiss was designed to give comfort, to rediscover, to seduce.

It wasn't a kiss she'd received from Tyce before and Sage didn't know how to respond. She wanted to urge him to deepen it, to take more, to stoke the fire but she also didn't want the sweetness of this kiss to end. It was pure seduction, totally charming. And over far too soon. Tyce lifted his mouth off hers and leaned back, his black eyes glinting in the low light of the room. Sage was surprised to see the fine tremor in the hand he put back on her thigh.

"Seeing you fall... You scared the crap out of me, Sage."

Her words had deserted her so Sage just nodded, unable to drop her eyes from the emotional thunderstorm in his eyes. It was the first time she'd seen Tyce without his reticent cloak, his barriers. There was so much emotion in those dark depths that it made her breath hitch, her heart rate accelerate.

Her hand lifted to touch his face. She longed to run her hands down his big biceps, to pull his shirt up and feel the definition in his chest. She wanted to crawl inside him, explore that steel-trap mind, his creative genius, peek into his soul. Tyce made her forget to keep her distance; he tempted her in ways that petrified her.

It was time to step back… Way back.

"So, the phone calls," she said, her voice curt.

At her prosaic words, his shields came up. "Everyone said they would come over tonight to check up on you, so instead of them arriving in dribs and drabs, I told Linc to tell them to come around after work and to stay for dinner."

Sage nodded, resigned. Sure, they were worried about her but she knew that her brothers wanted another chance to check up on Tyce, to see if he was treating her right and to, possibly, drop another threat or two in his ear.

One day they'd wake up and realize that Tyce marched to the beat of his own drum and didn't really care what they thought.

Sage ran a hand over her face, pain pounding through her head and her tailbone and her arm in symphony. "They'll want food and I don't have much in the fridge. I'll have to order in."

Tyce squeezed her thigh to get her attention. "I made a chicken casserole and there's more than enough for everybody."

Sage frowned at him. "You cook?"

"I do."

"Since when?"

"Since I was a kid and the only way to get a good meal into my stomach, and more important, into Lachlyn's, was to learn," Tyce shot back and immediately looked annoyed that he'd allowed something so personal to slip.

Sage knew that he didn't want to pursue this conversation but since he'd opened the door, she was going to walk through it. She was just…doing a background check on him, she told herself. Finding out information about her baby's father.

Pffft. Even she didn't believe the garbage she was thinking! The truth was that Tyce fascinated her. And, yet again, she was venturing where she shouldn't go.

Oh, well…

"Where was your mom? Didn't she feed you?"

"When she felt well enough to do so," Tyce replied, standing up. That action and his closed-off face was a sign—billboard high and painted in neon—that he wasn't discussing his past anymore. Or again.

"Was she sick?"

Tyce stared at the abstract painting above her head and he eventually shrugged. "She suffered from depression. There were days when she wouldn't get up off the floor, when she'd rock herself for hours. Most days, she managed to work—just—but when she got home she'd collapse into a nonresponsive heap. If I didn't look after myself, feed myself, and Lachlyn when she came along, we didn't eat. It was… Yeah, it was tough."

"Where is she now? Is she…" Sage hesitated, keeping her voice neutral, knowing that she had to be careful how she framed her questions. If she was too blasé she'd sound callous; if she came across as being too sympathetic Tyce would immediately stop talking. "…still alive?"

"She died from a bout of pneumonia a long time ago."

Sage pulled her bottom lip between her teeth. "I'm so sorry, Tyce."

Tyce shrugged. "It happened."

When he looked around the room, Sage knew that he was trying to change the subject. She wasn't surprised. Tyce had told her more in ten minutes than he'd shared the entire time they'd been together three years ago. He resumed his seat next to her on the bed and picked a curl up off her cheek and pushed it behind her ear. "I keep looking at that photo of the red diamond flower ring. It's amazing. It's your time to spill. Tell me about it and tell me why you didn't want it displayed at the exhibition."

And this was the price she had to pay: she'd peeked under the lid of his Pandora's box and he thought he could do the same. Damn the person who'd invented the concept of tit for tat.

Sage sighed, pushed the rest of her wayward hair behind her ears and looked at a spot behind his head.

She eventually looked at him again. "How much do you know about red diamonds?"

"Not much. That they are rare? That they are phenomenally expensive?"

Sage nodded. "There are only around twenty to thirty true red diamonds in the world and most are less than half a carat. My father was, like Jaeger, a gem hunter and my mom often accompanied him on his trips. He bought that diamond from a Brazilian farmer and it's, as far as we know, the largest red diamond in the world. It was his biggest find, ever, and I remember how excited they, and Connor, were. My mom assumed that the stone would be sold but my dad wanted to give it to my mom to celebrate their tenth wedding anniversary. Connor designed and made the ring. The flower petals represent each of her children."

Tyce frowned. "There are four petals but only three of you."

Sadness passed through Sage's expressive eyes. "My mom was pregnant with her fourth child when she died."

Tyce swore and rubbed a hand over his face. He then slipped his hand around the back of her neck and he rested his forehead against hers. "Now it's my turn to say I'm sorry."

Sage managed a small smile. "One of my clearest memories is of her looking at that stone, holding it up to the light, a soft smile on her face. She was utterly entranced by it. She would've loved the ring." A small laugh left her lips. "The stone was worth millions and millions but my father was prepared to give it to my mother because she loved it so much. They were like that, you know. People before things, before money."

And, because she was such a scaredy-cat when it came to men and relationships, she would never have what her parents experienced. She'd never know what a soul-deep connection felt like. Maybe this baby would make her better, stronger, more courageous. Maybe, in a year or two or ten, she'd manage to move past her fears, stop equating love with loss and take a chance.

It wouldn't be with Tyce; loving him wasn't an option. Despite their mind-blowing sexual connection, he'd never settle down, not the way that she imagined she'd need him to. Like Connor, a relationship was way down his list of priorities.

"Does the general public know about the stone or should I write a promise in blood that I will never reveal its existence?" Tyce asked, his eyes glinting with amusement.

"Get a sharp knife and a piece of paper." Of everything she had to worry about, Tyce talking out of turn wasn't a concern. She trusted him. He wasn't the type to blab.

"I used another red diamond for the Ballantyne photo shoot, explaining that it was my mom's favorite stone but not explaining why. I didn't want to use the ring because it would've generated a tsunami of publicity. I just wanted to remember it—think about

"FAST FIVE" READER SURVEY

Your participation entitles you to:
* ✷ 4 Thank-You Gifts Worth Over $20!

Complete the survey in minutes.

Get 2 FREE Books

Your Thank-You Gifts include **2 FREE BOOKS** and **2 MYSTERY GIFTS**. There's no obligation to purchase anything!

See inside for details.

Dear Reader,

Since you are a lover of our books, your opinions are important to us... and so is your time.

That's why we made sure your **"FAST FIVE" READER SURVEY** can be completed in just a few minutes. Your answers to the five questions will help us remain at the forefront of women's fiction.

And, as a thank-you for participating, we'd like to send you **4 FREE THANK-YOU GIFTS!**

Enjoy your gifts with our appreciation,

Pam Powers

To get your
4 FREE THANK-YOU GIFTS:

✴ Quickly complete the "Fast Five" Reader Survey
and return the insert.

it—as a stone my mom loved, part of a ring my dad had made for her, a symbol of the family he adored."

Tyce's thumb stroked her jaw. "I can understand that. Your parents sound like they were good people, Sage."

She nodded as he thumbed away a tear that sneaked out of the corner of her eye. "They really were, Tyce. So was Connor. I know that Connor got your mom pregnant but if he'd known about Lachlyn he would've…"

Tyce placed a kiss against her temple. "Ssh, sweetheart. It's okay, Sage."

It wasn't, but here, half lying against Tyce's chest, she felt like it could be. She felt like nothing could hurt her, that there was a strong wall between her and life's next hard slap. Yeah, she definitely felt safe, Sage thought, her eyes drooping closed.

Dammit. That wasn't good.

She should push away, should push *him* away, make him go, but she didn't have the strength or the inclination. She just wanted to lie here, soaking in Tyce's heat and strength and allow herself to drift off to sleep.

Eight

Three days later, Sage sat on the corner of her sofa, her feet on an ottoman. Tyce was still with her and he was clearing up after dinner. He was a fabulous cook, far better than she was. She glanced down at the papers on her lap and wrinkled her nose. Depending on the answers to the surveys she held in her hand, Tyce might even be a better parent than her...

When they had started to talk about the baby, they both, swiftly, realized that the real work started once the baby was born and that they had no idea what they were doing. They both knew how to change a diaper and make a bottle; Sage had looked after her nephews often enough for the mechanics to sink in and Tyce remembered changing and feeding Lachlyn when he was little more than a kid himself. They'd agreed that, because the baby would be raised in two separate homes, they needed a consensus on how the logistics would work, on what mattered and what didn't, what lines couldn't be crossed.

Not knowing how to start, they'd turned to the net.

Sage felt Tyce's breath on her cheek and she looked up to see him leaning down, his mouth close to her ear. "Do you think these parenting surveys are a good idea?"

Sage looked into his eyes and she shrugged. "I don't know. But I think they would give us an idea of our different parenting styles. I think I'll be more of an operate-from-instinct type of parent and I suspect that you will be the disciplined one."

"What makes you say that?"

"Oh, the fact that you do Tai Chi at the crack of dawn, you go to the dojo four times a week and that you run six miles a day."

"Eight," Tyce corrected her and Sage saw the flash of the dimple in his cheek as the corners of his mouth lifted. Then she noticed that he was holding a bag of frozen peas, which he dropped into her lap.

"Slap it against your tailbone and that bruise," he told her, holding a glass of red wine in his other hand.

Sage tried to twist her waist so that the bag of peas hit the right spot but winced when she turned. While she wasn't in as much pain as she had been the evening of the accident, she was still damned sore. Tyce whipped the bag from her hand.

"Can you lean forward a bit?" he asked her, his big hand on her shoulder.

Sage leaned forward so that he could slide the bag down her back. She winced again as the cold seeped through the fabric of her yoga pants. With her injuries, yoga pants, a snug sports top and hoodie was all Tyce had seen her in. Super casual wasn't her best look. "Damn, I'm not sure what's worse, the cold or the bruise."

Tyce sat down next to her, his muscled thigh pressing into hers, and her body started to tingle. "Trust me, the bruise is worse," Tyce said.

"That bad?" she asked. After all, she couldn't see it herself.

"Size of a football and a deep, angry blue," Tyce told her. "You hit the ground at speed."

He snagged a copy of the survey from her lap and squinted at the paper. "Okay, let's do this. Question one… Is diaper changing a job for the mom, the dad or both of you?" His lips twitched. "That's easy. If it's loaded, it's your job."

"And if I'm not with you?" Sage asked, feeling the heat from his body, his fresh, citrus-masculine-Tyce smell drifting up her nose. Her sensitive nipples tightened and her blood slowly heated.

"The kid will have to hold it," Tyce replied before flashing her one of his sexy, oh-so-rare grins. "I'm kidding. I'll do my share but, fair warning, I'll try and charm you into doing it if I can. If I can't charm you, I might resort to begging."

He'd probably succeed too, Sage thought as drops of water from the frozen packet of peas ran down her butt and she twisted her arm, wanting to pull the bag away.

Tyce placed his hand on hers and shook his head. "Five more minutes. Please?"

Sage pulled her hand out from under his and gave him a reluctant nod. Tyce's hand moved up to her shoulder so she partially spun around so that the back of her head rested on his chest. She looked down at her sheet of paper.

"The two most important qualities I want my child to possess? Mmm, that's hard."

Tyce didn't hesitate. "Resilience and determination."

Sage nodded, immediately understanding that his childhood would've been even more difficult if he hadn't been blessed with enormous doses of those traits.

"You?" Tyce asked.

Sage bit the inside of her lip. "I'd like our child to be bold and courageous. To have confidence."

"Just like her, or his, mama."

Sage tipped her head back, saw the warmth in his eyes and wanted to explain that she wasn't bold, or brave. She was scared to live life to the fullest, scared of what life had in store for her, scared to love, to open herself up and feel. She wanted to tell Tyce that her default habit was to run from people and situations that made her feel uncomfortable, that every day she spent with him was a curious combination of terror and exhilaration. He made her feel alive, like she was plugged into an unseen source of energy that replenished and renewed. She also had a knot in her stomach because she knew that this couldn't last, her bruises would fade and Tyce would move back to the periphery of her life, leaving her feeling empty and alone.

Sage saw Tyce swallow, noticed that he clutched the paper a little tighter, felt the tension radiating off him. He cleared his throat and when he spoke his voice was a low growl. "Next question... I know my partner is going to be a wonderful parent because...*hell*."

Sage faced him and she caught the fear in his eyes, the flicker of insecurity that crossed his face. She frowned. "Wait... Do you not think that you will be a good parent?"

Tyce's expression changed to inscrutability and, because she did it herself, Sage knew that it was his way of retreating, silently telling her that he didn't want to continue this discussion. She took the piece of paper from his hand, dropped it, and the bag of peas, to the floor. She turned to face him and placed her hand on his heart and felt the thud-thud-thud of his heart beneath her palm. "Why on earth would you think that?"

Tyce took a long time to answer. "Because I had a crappy upbringing? Because I never had chance to be a child so I have no idea how to relate to one? How am I going to deal with a child when I can barely tolerate people?"

"You seem to be able to tolerate me," Sage pointed out.

Tyce raked his hand through his hair. "Yeah, well, you...you're the exception to the rule."

It would be easy to make a joke in order to lighten the mood, to push away the cloud of emotion hanging over their heads. But Sage didn't want to, not this time, this *one* time. Sage lifted her hand to run her fingers along his jaw. "Tyce, you're a man who steps up to the plate, who accepts his responsibilities, who does the right thing. Sure, you're not the most voluble person in the world but, when you speak, you always have something valuable to say. You're intelligent and talented—" her fingers drifted over his mouth and she handed him a small smile "—and you're hot. Our baby will be just fine and you will be too."

Tyce felt her words wash over him, as restorative as soft, soaking summer rain. Funny how, with a few words, Sage could make him miss something he'd never had. He'd read so many positive reviews, was the recipient of numerous awards, a million kudos about his art, but he'd never been complimented for the man he was. It made his stomach flip, his heart pound, his soul sigh.

It definitely lowered his resistance to her, made him want to throw caution to the wind and take what he constantly craved. Tyce allowed his thumb to drift across her chin and slide across her full bottom lip but if he kissed her now he wouldn't be able to stop. He'd pull her clothes off her spectacular body and he'd kiss every patch of her skin, starting with her mouth and ending with her toes. He'd wait until she was writhing with need, unable to remember her own name, wait until she was screaming his before sliding into her and pitching them into oblivion.

He wanted her with an intensity that rocked him to his core.

Sage leaned forward, curled her fingers around his neck and rested her forehead on his cheekbone. Sparks skittered through him. "Make love to me, Tyce. Just once more."

She'd echoed his thoughts, subconsciously picking up on his burning desire. Tyce groaned and shook his head. "It's not a good idea, Sage. You're still bruised and it'll make the situation, us, so much more complicated."

"I need not to think, I need to step out of my head," Sage murmured. "You can do that for me because you're the only one who can."

"You're hurt—"

"I'm fine and I want you. I want to remember how good we were together and I want to forget all the complications, just for a little while. You're the best medicine for what ails me, Tyce."

He shouldn't; this wasn't a good idea. They had a child to raise together, a life to navigate as co-parents and friends, hearts to protect.

"Making love to you always made me feel centered, stronger, better. Make me feel like that again, Tyce."

He was just a man and not half as strong as he thought he was. Hell, around Sage, he wasn't strong at all. She made him *feel*, made him ache, made him step out from behind his walls. He shouldn't do this;

it wasn't smart but, like her, he was throbbing with need, desperate to have her and taste her, to lose himself in her.

Just once.

Tyce watched caution fly away on the wind as his mouth touched hers. Her lips immediately opened and he swept his tongue inside, and then he was riding the storm. Yeah, this, *Sage*, her hand against his chest, the fingers of her other hand raking through his hair, was what he couldn't resist. Her mouth was pure sugar-spice and he could kiss her until time fizzled away.

He needed to take this slow, Tyce reminded himself as he unzipped the front of her hoodie. He eased the sides apart and left her lips long enough to pull his head back so that he could look at her. Her nipples were pushing through the fabric of her sports top and he had to taste one bud. He pulled the stretchy fabric down and sucked her nipple into his mouth, laving her with his tongue before taking her in even deeper. She felt so amazing, familiar yet different.

Sage was making those little breathy moans that turned him steel hard. Tyce pushed her hoodie off and lifted her top up and over her head. He tossed both to the floor, gently pushing her back so that she lay flat on the couch.

Putting his hands on either side of her head, he looked down into her lovely face. "Are you okay? Sure you want to do this?"

"Yes and I'm fine."

She wasn't; he could see a little pain under her passion. "Tell me if you want to stop."

Sage's low laugh danced over his skin. "Not a chance." She tapped his chest. "You have too many clothes on, Latimore."

Tyce sat back, pulled his T-shirt over his head and sucked in his breath when Sage's hand ran over a pec, across a nipple and over his stomach. She tugged at the band of his jeans. "Off."

"You first." Tyce slid his hands along her back, across her hips, his thumbs hooking the band of her yoga pants and pulling them down. He looked at the tiny triangle of fabric covering her secret, feminine places and couldn't help his eyes moving up, to her stomach. He hauled in a breath and placed a hot, openmouthed kiss on her tiny baby bump, before placing his ear on her stomach.

Sage's hand touched his hair and he knew that she was also thinking of their baby, the fact that they'd made another person doing what they did best, and that was loving each other... Giving each other pleasure.

Talking about pleasure, Tyce pulled up and back. He'd heard Sage's hiss of pain when she lifted her butt to take off her pants and he had no intention of hurting her again. He'd have to be creative making love to her and that was okay; creativity was one of his strongest traits.

Tyce slipped his fingers under the thin bands of her thong and twisted, snapping first one side of her panties and then the other. His heart beating a million miles per minute, he pulled the fabric from between her legs and then Sage was naked, looking as beautiful as he'd ever seen her.

He just looked and then looked some more, his concentration breaking when Sage's hand danced across her stomach and headed lower. Oh, hell, no, giving her pleasure was his job.

Tyce quickly shucked his pants, his mind swirling with possibilities. Missionary sex was out, as was her kneeling on top of him. Hell, he doubted that he'd even get inside her but that was okay. Giving Sage pleasure, rocketing her to an orgasm, was more important than him getting off.

Naked now, Tyce slid his fingers between her folds, dazed by her wet warmth. It was such a turn-on to know she wanted him as much as he wanted her. They'd messed up so often but this truly was what they did best.

Sage's fingers pressed his onto her most sensitive spot. "I need you, Tyce. I need this."

Her low, slow and sexy words sent more blood, if that was possible, to his already throbbing erection. Sage's hand moved to her side and she encircled him and Tyce was quite certain that if she kept up that squeezing, stroking action, he'd lose it.

But, judging by her trembling limbs and her flushed body, her desperate eyes, Sage was hovering on the edge, as well. Tyce moved so that he was looming over her, his arms holding his weight off her. Positioning himself, he rubbed her, his shaft sliding over that bundle of nerves. Sage moaned her approval and he repeated the action, loving her heat and the friction and hell, just being close to her. Being inside her would be better but this was almost as good. Tyce lifted one hand and pushed her hair out of her eyes, wanting to watch her climb. Her eyes met his and he stepped into the deep, now-foggy blue. She lifted her hips and he shook his head. "Let me do the work, sweetheart."

"Then get on with it," Sage hissed.

God, he'd forgotten how demanding she could be when she was on the brink and he wasn't giving her what she wanted. In the past he'd loved to tease her, taking her, and her temper, higher until she shattered in his arms.

She was on the brink now, so close. And so was he. Unable to resist, Tyce pushed himself between her legs, sliding into her hot tight channel, keeping her legs together so that she didn't put any more pressure on her coccyx and bruises than necessary. She was hot and tight and he couldn't move the way he wanted to but he'd deal. He was inside Sage and he'd stepped into heaven.

Sage moaned and he gently thrust against her, short shallow strokes that were more erotic than he believed possible. Tyce rested his elbows on cushions next to her head. He cradled her face and kissed her, his tongue matching the rhythm of his hips.

He felt Sage's breath quicken, felt her tremble and then felt the gush of warmth against him, the tightening of her internal walls. That was all he needed and he tensed as pleasure rocketed through him. He groaned into Sage's mouth and then again, holding her tight as tremors passed from her body to his, his to hers.

While his brain and body patched itself back together, he stroked Sage's glorious frame and dropped gentle kisses on her mouth, her cheekbone, her jaw. His hand stopped when it reached her stomach and his big hand covered most of her slight bump.

His. The thought came from his heart and skittered through his body. The baby was his and so was she. Somehow, in whatever form they took, and on some level they would always be his.

The next morning, Sage stood in her shower and lifted her face up to receive a blast of hot water. She ached in places she didn't know she had, good places, places that had been long neglected. Her body felt like she'd spent the day at a spa, loose and relaxed.

Her mind felt like a turtle trying to walk through peanut butter.

Sage placed her hands on the wall of the shower cubicle and watched the water swirl around the drain. What were the implications of making love with Tyce? Was it a once-off thing? What did any of it, all of it, mean?

Sage closed her eyes in frustration and slapped her hand against the white tiles. What had happened to her ordered, calm life? Three months ago she felt calm and in charge and one night—one night!—with Latimore flipped everything around.

Tyce was an amazing lover, but he was also a

good man. Good seemed like a bland word but Sage thought it was underused and misunderstood. Good didn't mean rich or good-looking; it meant that someone was prepared to do the right thing, the honorable thing, to take the path less traveled, even if it flew in the face of convention. Good, to her, meant that he was responsible, honorable and honest.

She liked him…

Sage sighed. She'd forgotten how much she enjoyed his company out of the bedroom. She spoke more than he did but, over these past few days, Tyce held up his end of the conversation. They'd discussed movies and politics, books and, of course, art. Actually, they'd argued about art… Tyce, surprisingly, had a fondness for the Dutch Golden Age of painting, artists like Hals and van Baburen, and Sage preferred art from the twentieth century.

But whether they were talking art or music, spending time with Tyce was…fun. Stimulating and relaxing at the same time. She felt she could say anything to him and he wouldn't judge her. Connor was like that and Sage was reminded of how much alike they were. Strong, alpha, honorable men. Honest men… about everything. Including their antipathy toward relationships and commitment.

Like before, Tyce tempted her to open up, to give him more, to delve beneath the surface of her armor. That was still a very dangerous path to walk down and she couldn't allow herself to take it. She could not drop her shields and let him into her heart. That way lay hurt, disappointment and madness. Tyce had the power, like nobody she'd ever encountered before, to turn her life upside down. Loving and then losing him would devastate her and having to interact with him as they raised a child together would be like trying to dodge asteroid strikes while walking through the last level of hell.

Frankly, that scenario was best to be avoided. If she was smart she'd say thanks for the fun time and push him out of her apartment and her life. She'd done it with other men, not many, and she could do it with Tyce. But she didn't want to. She wanted more sex, more conversations and yes, she thought as her stomach growled, more of his fabulous cooking.

Maybe she could have a fling with him. She could enjoy his body and his mind and when they ran out of steam, which they would, she'd revert back to being friends and co-parents because she'd been sensible and kept her heart out of their interactions.

She could do that, she decided. Connor told her she could do anything she wanted to...

Okay, maybe he hadn't been thinking of her in terms of her having a no strings fling when he imparted those words of wisdom. But she was a smart, modern woman and like millions of smart, modern women she knew that the act of sex was not a declaration of love, commitment or anything other than the giving and receiving of pleasure.

She could keep her heart out of the equation and stay emotionally protected.

Couldn't she?

Nine

Tyce looked around as Sage finally made an appearance the next morning. She looked better than she had last night, but her walk down the cast-iron staircase suggested that she was still feeling a little stiff. Standing at her sloping windows, he watched her as she headed straight for the coffee machine, her eyes foggy from sleep. They'd only been together a few weeks so long ago but some things hadn't changed: the great sex, obviously, the fact that she squeezed toothpaste from the middle of the tube and that her brain didn't start to work properly until after nine and three cups of coffee, now decaffeinated because of the baby.

Tyce looked at his watch. It was bang on nine and he'd been up since five, had gone to his warehouse to pick up clothes and returned here before six. He'd then pushed back her furniture and done an hour of Tai Chi before heading outside for a run. Sage was barely functional.

Tyce walked across the room, his bare feet making no sound on the wooden floors. "Morning," he said, stopping a foot from Sage's turned back.

Sage yelped, squealed and groaned. She turned around quickly and, hand on her heart, scowled at him. "Holy crap, Latimore! Scare me to death, why don't you?"

"Sorry."

Stepping around her, Tyce reached for a cup from the cupboard above the coffee machine and placed it beneath the spout of the machine. He hit a button and the air between them filled with the rich scents of very expensive coffee. For the last few years he'd been living on a budget, curtailing his expenses, but good coffee was one of the few luxuries he'd been unable to deny himself.

Sex with Sage, as he'd decided last night when she lay across his chest, damp and boneless, was another of the necessities of life he couldn't do without. Speaking of, it had been too long since he'd last kissed her...

Tyce was just about to place his hands on her hips, lower his mouth to hers, when she spoke.

"So, I supposed we'd better talk about what happened last night."

Ugh. He really didn't want to. Tyce succumbed to his urge to touch and hooked his hand around her neck, using his thumb to tip her face upward. "I always prefer action to discussion."

Sage half smiled. "I know you do but I think that, three years ago, one of our faults was that we spent too much time making love and not nearly enough time talking."

Tyce mock frowned at her. "FYI, a man can never spend enough time in bed."

"Duly noted." Sage placed her hands on his chest and pushed away. "But, sorry for you, I do have something to say."

Dammit, Tyce thought, stepping back. *Here it comes... I don't think this is a good idea; we shouldn't complicate the situation; I've got a lot on my plate.* He was expecting at least one excuse for them not to continue sleeping together, possibly all three.

"Are you interested in having more sex with me?"

Hot damn. Was that even a serious question? Judging by the traces of insecurity he saw in her eyes and the tremor in her voice, it sure sounded like one. Hell, yes, he wanted to sleep with her again. As many times as was humanly possible. "Uh... Yes?"

"You don't sound too sure," Sage replied.

"Trust me, I'm damn sure," Tyce growled. "What's this about, Sage?"

Sage placed her hand over the rim of her cup and rolled the cup on the counter. "Well, we can do that, if you want."

Holy crap. "Is that something you want too, Sage?"

He knew it was but he suddenly needed the words. "Yes. But…"

Yes. It was a small-sounding word but it had huge consequences. He was going to have her again, and soon. As soon as she gave him the green light he'd kiss her and then he'd pull that thin cashmere jersey off her slim frame and he'd flip open the button to her jeans. They'd be naked and on the way to heaven.

"But it can't be more than sex, Tyce," Sage said, rushing her words. "It's what we're good at. The rest of the stuff, we aren't good at that." She crossed her arms and rocked on her heels. "I don't want to be hurt again, Tyce. I don't want to hurt you."

"I hear you, Sage. I don't want to hurt you either. But we don't have to label this, define this. We don't have to put on restrictions, shove what we have into a box. No expectations, no pressure," Tyce told her. "We're just two people who think the other is hot, who are having a baby together and who are now sleeping together."

Tyce couldn't help but notice the relief in her eyes but sighed at the worry one layer down. Sage was still so damn vulnerable, and he'd have to be careful with her and for her. He'd have to be the one who kept an eye on how far and fast this went because there was, no matter what he said, always the possibility of this situation blowing up in their faces. They had a baby to raise together and they couldn't do that effectively if they ended up hating or resenting each other.

It was important that he looked at this situation

clearly. He'd been alone for so damn long, hell, he'd spent his life alone and he didn't know how to make the emotional connections that people needed. Only now, as an adult, did he realize how tired and drained he was when he was younger from constantly living in a state of fight-or-flight. Yeah, he'd take Sage's offer of sex—what man wouldn't?—but he'd put himself in a situation of feeling out of control and desperate.

But, for now, he'd enjoy her, take what she was so generously offering because making love with Sage was earth-shattering.

Tyce lifted his hand to touch her, to connect, but she shook her head and stepped out of his reach. Damn, she wasn't done talking…

"I know that we are equally responsible for me being pregnant but I have this crazy urge to apologize, to say sorry for messing up your life with a baby."

God. That was what she was thinking? That her being pregnant was something he regretted? Man, she couldn't be more wrong. He regretted many things, particularly his inability to be the type of man she needed, but he had no regrets about their still-baking baby.

Maybe that was because he was starting to see their child as a bridge back to some sort of normality, a way to modify his ideas about families and what they meant. He was being given a second chance, as an adult, to create a unit that had all the people in all the right roles. He and Sage wouldn't live together but his child would have a mother and a father and they would be the adults and their child would have the freedom to be a child.

And yes, maybe he was looking at this baby as the one soul with whom he could reconnect emotionally; a safe place to try that. His kid would be *his* kid, would be a big part of his life for the next eighteen years at least, right?

Tyce placed his hands on either side of Sage's face, thinking that her skin was so soft, that she smelled like a field of gently scented roses. Her blue eyes locked on his and he took a step so that her breasts just touched his chest. He needed to get closer, needed to feel her in his arms, needed... God, he needed her. His head started to swim but he knew he couldn't afford to be distracted; his answer was too important to mess up. "We've made a muddle of a lot of things, Sage, but you having my baby? That's not one of them."

"Are you sure? He, or she, is going to flip our world."

"That's not always a bad thing and I'm strapped in for the ride." He kissed her nose before pulling her closer, hugging her tight. "The baby is a gift that I haven't said thank you for so...thank you. I have many regrets, Sage, but this baby will never be one of them."

Tyce felt a little of her tension seep out of her body so he lowered his head and slowly, gently kissed the corner of her mouth, leaving his lips there, inhaling her unique scent. This time he allowed his head to swim, and placed a hand in the middle of her back and pulled her up against his body, his erection pushing into her stomach, her breasts against his chest. Sage sighed and once again he slowly, gently traced the seam of her mouth, the edges of her lips. He wanted to plunge and plunder, to allow their crazy passion to spiral but he knew that if he let passion reign, he'd lose her.

This was a kiss of promise, of tenderness, something different than what they'd ever shared before. This wasn't the time, he reminded his junk, to do what came naturally. That time would come later and he could wait. This moment was too important to mess up.

Tyce pulled back and then stepped away from her, running his hands through his hair. He risked looking at Sage. She held her fingers to her lips, her eyes wide and dreamy. Tyce started to move toward her, caught himself and muttered a silent curse.

His sensible side surfaced. If he didn't corral his emotional side he would create that which would be forever difficult to tame. Later, he could love her when emotion wasn't running quite so high, when his heart wasn't trying to punch its way out of his chest. Yeah, it was better if they calmed down a little.

Or a lot.

Sage had run out of excuses to delay meeting Lachlyn. She'd deliberately missed a dinner at The Den to introduce Lachlyn to the clan and she'd postponed meeting her for coffee. Twice. Her excuses were so thin they had holes in them. Giving in to verbal pressure from her brothers, and subtle, silent pressure from Tyce, Sage finally asked Tyce's sister to meet her at The Den. Linc and Tate and their kids were out of town so she had her childhood home to herself and she thought it was the right place for their first meeting.

Sage stepped into the hallway of the famous brownstone and started to unwrap her scarf. "Maybe we should've met at a coffee shop."

Tyce, who'd offered to accompany her to The Den and stay to introduce them before leaving them to talk, didn't reply. He just stood in the double-volume hallway, his eyes darting around the magnificent space. Tyce was another reason why she couldn't delay meeting Lachlyn any longer. The newest member of the clan was his sister and she couldn't keep avoiding her baby's aunt.

Despite her excuses not to meet Lachlyn, Sage could admit to feeling a tad braver, a little stronger about the changing circumstances. Also, being around Tyce made her feel like she should step up a bit more. He was consistently strong and she was not talking about that most very excellent body she adored. He was mentally tough and if they were going to co-parent together, be in each other's lives, she had to be, as well.

She wanted to be the best version of herself, for her baby, obviously, but also for Tyce.

"Are you okay, Sage?"

Sage darted a look at him and shrugged. Was she?

This was a little similar to an adopted child meeting her biological mother for the first time. "I'm nervous, jittery, excited, nauseous."

Tyce's smile touched his sexy mouth. "She's feeling the same."

"You should be with her, Tyce. This is a big deal for her," Sage said, feeling guilty.

"Lach is an excited nervous but you're a terrified nervous," Tyce replied. "Lachlyn isn't going to run like a rabbit but you might."

True. *Will she like me?* Sage placed a hand on her stomach. *Will I like her? Will she get my jokes?* God, she really hoped Lachlyn had a sense of humor. *Would she ask to borrow money or clothes or, God, jewels? No, of course she wouldn't, this was Tyce's sister, for goodness' sake, and Tyce wouldn't have raised her to think like that.*

Will she like me? Will I like her?

Now she was repeating her thoughts and totally losing it. Sage glanced at her watch, a minute to go, if Lachlyn was the prompt type.

"Take a breath, Sage."

"Why am I doing this?"

"I'm presuming that's a rhetorical question?" Tyce asked, his hands in the pockets of his leather jacket.

"Lachlyn might fly into my life, hang around and then disappear again."

Tyce walked over to her and rubbed his hands up and down her arms. "Why would you think that?"

"Because that's what people do!" She frowned.

"What if we bonded, if we came to love each other and she died? Of cancer or in a helicopter crash?"

"Dramatic much, Sage? She's an archivist—she deals with documents. She might die from falling off a ladder or after being buried by falling boxes but she won't die from a helicopter crash."

Sage frowned at her lover. "You're mocking me."

"Just a little."

He didn't understand and he probably never would. Sure, she sounded like a drama queen but she'd had her life wrenched apart; she'd experienced death and desolation. She knew that bad things happened when they were least expected to.

She couldn't do this, she thought. She couldn't let Lachlyn in. Sage picked up her coat from where she'd tossed it onto the chaise lounge to the left of the door. She shoved her arm into a sleeve. If she hurried, she could leave before Lachlyn arrived.

The heavy chimes of the doorbell rang through the hallway and, looking through the glass inserts, Sage saw a tiny blonde standing outside, her chin pushed into the folds of a pink scarf.

Lachlyn was here, actually here. Suddenly Sage didn't know what to do or what to say. Her eyes flew to Tyce's face and she lifted up her hands. "Will you stay?"

"Are you sure that's what you want?"

"Please?"

"Hang on a sec, Lach," Tyce called out. He stepped up to Sage and cupped the back of her head with his large hand, pulling her forehead to his chest.

His head dropped and Sage heard his rumbling, sexy voice close to her ear.

"She's just as scared as you are. Like you, she just wants to be liked. She also just wants to know about her dad, this family. She's the interloper here, Sage. This is your house, your family. There's no reason for you to be scared."

"I don't like letting people in, Tyce." It was a massive admission and Sage wondered if he'd understand that she wasn't talking about this house or her family but about letting people into her life.

"Me neither, honey. But neither can we stay the same. We have to learn and we have to grow. And we can only do that by allowing new people and new experiences into our lives." Tyce dropped a kiss into her hair. "She's a nice person, Sage. You could come to love her."

And that was the problem, Sage thought. Loving someone was fine—she could do that. She just didn't want to deal with the fallout when they stopped loving her and disappeared from her life in whatever form that took.

"Open the door, honey," Tyce said, stepping away and giving her an encouraging smile. "You've got this."

Sage shook her head. She really didn't feel like she did.

Thank God, the first official, welcome-to-the-family-Lachlyn dinner was over and Sage could finally go home.

She looked around the crowded hallway of The Den, thinking of so many other dinners they'd ended here in a flurry of goodbyes. Connor always stood to the left of the imposing front door, the last person they saw before leaving the house.

Changes, Sage thought, yanking her coat belt tighter. God, she hated them.

"If you pull that any tighter you're going to cut off your air supply," Tyce told her, putting his hand on hers.

Sage, irritated, swatted his hand away. "I've been tying my coat for a while now."

"What is your problem?" Tyce asked, keeping his voice low. "You've been scratchy all evening."

Where to start? Instead of answering him, she looked around the hallway and swallowed the compressed ball of emotion in her throat. She'd barely had time to recover, to digest her meeting with Lachlyn this afternoon when Linc had sprung this family dinner on her, blithely explaining that he'd already sent Tyce an invitation and thereby taking the decision about inviting him to accompany her out of her hands.

Would she have asked him? Probably not. After the meeting with Lachlyn, which had been emotional and difficult, she'd realized how easy it was to rely on Tyce's steady presence and his strength. Counting on Tyce was a dangerous habit to slide into. He was her lover, sure, but she refused to fall in love with him and relying on him for anything other than help to raise their child was foolish. She was setting herself up for an almighty fall and that had to stop immediately.

Having Tyce with her, in The Den, made her feel like they were imposters, acting a role. They were sleeping together; they were not in a relationship and she didn't like all the side-eye she'd received from her family whenever Tyce put his arm around her shoulder and his hand on her knee. They were not a couple and he had no right to give her family the impression that they were.

Sage looked around at the faces she loved best. Beck had his arms around Cady's waist, his chin resting on her shoulder. Jaeger was holding Ty and Piper was tucked into his side. Tate's hand was on Shaw's head and Ellie was asleep, her beautiful face on Tate's shoulder. Love streamed out of Tate's eyes every time she looked at Linc.

Oh, damn, every time she spent time with her brothers and their wives, she started to think that she might want the love they'd found. And that was the real source of her irritation. She started thinking about how it would feel to walk out of this house with her hand in Tyce's, heading back to their place, content in the idea that they were creating a family within a family.

Even if she was prepared to take a chance on love—she wasn't but this was all hypothetical—Tyce wasn't the man to give it to her.

He didn't want to immerse himself in a relationship like her brothers had; he didn't want the day-to-day interactions, the ups and the downs. He wanted to be their baby's father and, for as long as it worked between them, for them to sleep together. When that stopped, when the passion faded away, he would too.

But the more time she spent with him, the more she was at risk of feeling more for him than she should, the more she wanted what her sisters-in-law had: a strong, sexy man standing at her side, ready to go to war for and with her.

Too many *more*s, she thought.

She had to readjust her thinking. Pronto.

Sage looked at Lachlyn and saw that Linc had his arm around her shoulders. Her big brother was scooping another lost Ballantyne chick under his arm. It was what he did so why was her throat closing, why did she feel like she was being pushed out of her own family?

Oh, God, how old was she? Thirteen?

"I need to go home," she muttered, walking toward the front door.

"Sage, wait!" Linc said and Sage heard the note of excitement in his voice. Wondering what he was about to slap her with now, Sage briefly rested her forehead on the door before turning around. Linc stood on the first step of the staircase and Lachlyn, tiny and blonde, stood next to him.

The hallway fell silent and Sage looked around at the faces she loved best. Sage darted a glance at Tyce and saw that his obsidian eyes were looking at her with a small frown. He seemed to be trying to look into her soul and she didn't like it. He had no right to do that; his having access to her body didn't mean that he was allowed to walk around her mind.

She didn't like any of it. Her world wasn't just changing, it was morphing into something different right before her eyes and she had no control over what was happening.

"So, as a welcome-to-the-family gift, Lachlyn," Linc said, "we thought that you might like Connor's favorite ring."

We? What *we*? She hadn't been consulted about giving anything of Connor's to Lachlyn! And his favorite ring? The one Sage and Connor had spent hours together designing and making since the bands of amber, pieces of an ancient meteorite and platinum, had required careful workmanship?

What the hell?

"He said that it was his all-time favorite ring," Linc continued. "He designed and made it and wore it every day."

Excuse me? She'd spent as many hours on that ring as Connor had. Maybe more. Sage watched as Linc handed Lachlyn the ring and blinked back tears.

So this was sharing, she thought. Her home, her brothers, the memories of her father. Frankly, it sucked.

God, what a day. She'd had enough.

Sage yanked open the door and stepped into the dark, tossing a cool, general good-night over her shoulder. She'd barely made it to the wrought iron gate when she felt Tyce take her hand. She immediately jerked her hand away and shoved it into her coat pocket.

"I didn't give her the ring, Sage."

"You brought her into our life," Sage whipped back. Direct hit, she realized, but she took no pleasure in the color draining from his face, the danger sparking in his eyes.

Tyce swallowed and looked away, and Sage knew that he was trying to control his temper. "I realize that this has been a tough day for you. It's not easy having someone come into your life, your family, and turn it upside down."

"This is all your fault," Sage said, her temper roiling and boiling. "You sought me out years ago as a way to connect with my family—"

"I explained that," Tyce said in a tight voice.

"Then you slept with me and bought millions of Ballantyne shares."

"You slept with me too."

Sage ignored him and dived deeper into her anger, knowing that she was lobbing accusations at his head when she most wanted to yell at him for not being able to give her what her brothers gave their wives.

Not that she could accept his love…

Sage knew that she was being irrational and that he was a handy target. It wasn't fair or right but if she didn't vent, she'd explode.

"Then you got me pregnant!" Sage shouted, her chest heaving.

"You forgot to blame me for poverty, climate change and the price of oil," Tyce said, gripping her biceps. He pulled in a slug of cold air and when he spoke his voice was calm. "Connor conceived Lachlyn so blame him. We are equally responsible for the pregnancy. This is all new, Sage, and you're scared. I get it. We're all picking our way through a minefield right now but yelling at each other isn't going to help.

"We've got to find a way to deal with this, with us, with the situation," Tyce added.

Sage desperately wanted to allow her tears to fall, to place her head against his chest and weep, taking strength from his arms. She wanted to kiss him, allow him to sweep her away from the here and now, to take her someplace where she didn't have to think of the baby, about the fact that she'd never have the emotional security that being in a committed relationship gave a person who was strong and brave enough to take that chance. She wasn't strong and she wasn't brave and she probably never would be.

"Just give Lachlyn a chance. Give this situation a chance. Let life unfold and trust that we'll all find our way."

Feeling sick and sad and still so very pissed off—anger was so much easier to deal with than fear—Sage lifted her chin and nailed Tyce with a sardonic look. "Get out of my head, Tyce. I never gave you permission to walk around in there. And keep your opinions about my family to yourself! You don't know us and you don't know what makes us tick. You don't know jack about what having a real family means!"

Tyce jerked his head back, clearly shocked. She

couldn't blame him; she sounded like a bitch on steroids. Her words had been designed to hurt and so unnecessary. Sage closed her eyes and held up her hand. Before she could apologize, Tyce turned around and started walking away.

Crap. Sage reached out and grabbed his elbow and he stopped.

"Tyce—"

Tyce's granite like expression killed the words in her throat. "I understand that you've had a rough day, Sage, but that doesn't mean that I get to be your verbal punch bag. I lived with a mother who was far better at that than you are but, as an adult, I no longer have to take the hits."

Dammit, she'd really angered him but, worse, she knew that she'd also hurt him. God, she felt ugly.

Tyce started to walk down the street, to the corner. "Where are you going?" Sage asked him.

"I'll hail a cab on the corner." He gestured to the cab that had pulled up next to them a few minutes before. "You take this one." Tyce nodded to her arm. "Your arm is fine and you don't need me hanging around all the time. We could probably both do with some space."

Tyce opened the cab door and gestured her inside. "Go home, Sage. We'll talk." He pushed his hand into his hair, his face expressionless.

"When?"

Tyce's smile held absolutely no warmth. "Oh, sometime between now and the baby's birth. Because, you know, I'm just the guy who knows nothing about anything, especially family."

Tyce slammed the door closed and Sage looked at him through the wet window. He turned his back on her and walked away, his broad back ramrod straight.

Sage felt a tear slide down her cheek and rested her temple on the glass of the window as the cab pulled away.

Her anger had nothing to do with Tyce and everything to do with her issues and her insecurities. She'd lashed out at him, projecting all her unhappiness in his direction. Had it been another subconscious attempt to push him away?

Probably, Sage admitted. But, because she'd been ugly and vicious and unfair, she'd hurt him. Sage felt humiliation and remorse roll through her.

And more than a little self-disgust.

Ten

Heavy rock blasting through the bottom floor of the warehouse, Tyce pushed up his welding helmet and frowned at the flicker of lights that was his version of a doorbell. It was past ten on a cold March night and, since few people knew of this address or that he lived here, he had no idea who was leaning on his doorbell. Dropping his welding rod and whipping off his helmet, he shoved his hands through his hair and walked across the cold concrete floor toward the small side door that stood adjacent to the huge roller doors.

Whipping the door open, he frowned at the small bundle of clothes stamping her feet on the sidewalk outside.

All he could see was big eyes and a pink nose. "Sage? What the hell?"

He opened the door wider and she hurried into the warehouse. She pulled her hands out of her pockets and started to unwind her scarf but he shook his head. "Upstairs. It's a hell of a lot warmer up there than it is down here."

Sage took the hand he held out and he pulled her toward the steel staircase that led to the second floor, which he'd converted into an apartment. Once inside, he started to unwind her scarf and helped her shrug out of her coat. Sage kept her eyes on his face and he wondered if she'd hoofed it across the Brooklyn Bridge to continue fighting with him. God, he hoped not. He didn't have the mental energy an argument required.

Tyce tossed her coat and scarf onto the chair next to the door and watched as Sage walked over to his fireplace and put her hands out to the fake flames. She sighed, slim shoulders lifting and falling. She turned around slowly, her eyes miserable when they met his.

Tyce tensed, waiting for the next blow to fall.

"I'm sorry. I was ugly and irrational and you have every right to be angry with me."

Tyce rubbed his lower jaw, stunned. An apology was the one statement he hadn't expected.

"Change scares me. Losing control terrifies me. Meeting Lachlyn was difficult and then we had the dinner—"

"You're a gorgeous, successful woman. Why

would meeting Lachlyn, who is as normal as can be, freak you out?"

"I keep people at a distance and if I feel like there is a chance of them getting closer than I feel comfortable with, I get anxious. And stressed. And then, as you saw, I freak out."

So that explained a thing or two. "Did you pick a fight in an attempt to push me away too?"

Sage nodded. "Yeah, probably. It's what I do best."

For the first time, Tyce saw her as she truly was, stripped down. She wasn't Sage, the Ballantyne princess or Sage, the wealthy, successful jewelry designer. She was just Sage, a woman who was facing incredible changes, whose life had been flipped upside down and inside out. Yeah, she'd been a bitch of epic proportions earlier but her insecurity, her churning emotion and her fears made her seem more real, more authentic.

Humbled by her apology, touched by her honesty, Tyce ducked his head and slapped his mouth across hers. He heard her intake of breath, felt her fighting the instinct to pull back and to step away from him but when he gently suckled on her bottom lip she fell toward him. Tyce wrapped his arms around her and hauled her in. Through the silk and cotton of their T-shirts, he could feel her hard nipples digging into his pecs and air rushed from his chest. Needing to feel her skin while he explored her mouth, he pushed his hand beneath the band of her leggings and his knees nearly buckled when he held her round but firm bottom in his hand.

He was kissing Sage and she was kissing him back, her tongue sliding into his mouth, tangling with his. Despite them making love frequently over the past two weeks, he still couldn't quite believe that she was back in his bed and his life. Tyce pulled her into him, his fingers sliding into the space between her legs and he could feel the moist heat from her core flowing over his skin.

She wanted him just as much as he wanted her and the thought made him feel as weak as a newborn and as strong as an ox. She was both his salvation and his destruction, his pleasure and his pain.

And he wanted her with all the ferocity of a winter's storm.

But that didn't mean that they should tumble into bed. They had a mountain to climb, a million words that they needed to exchange, issues to iron out. Their earlier fight was behind them and, now that he understood what fueled her anger, he found her humble and sincere apology easy to accept.

But he still had something to say. Tyce pulled back and stepped away from her, knowing that there was no way he'd get this out if he was touching her.

"Look, we're going to be in each other's lives for a long time—" he wanted to think forever and in every way possible but that wasn't likely "—and we need to be each other's best friends. That means being honest, about everything. If you feel sick or pissed off or overwhelmed, I want to know about it. And I'll be as open as I can…" Tyce took a deep breath. "That being said, there is something I should tell you."

"Okay. What?"

"This warehouse, it's all I have. I don't have that much money in the bank."

Sage, genuinely, didn't look like she cared. "Can I ask why?" she eventually asked. "You're, like, the highest paid artist in the world."

"Those Ballantyne shares are expensive, Sage. I haven't had much cash for the last couple of years. I've been living a lie. The Chelsea apartment? It's owned by one of my biggest clients who allowed me to crash there."

"That explains the lack of art, the lack of anything personal," Sage stated, looking remarkably sanguine. "I never liked that place. It wasn't you."

Tyce almost smiled at that; she'd hit the nail on the head. It really wasn't him. The real him was this place, redbrick and steel, a punch bag and a mat in the corner, welding machines and chain saws. It was comfortable couches and worn rugs. It was industrial Brooklyn, hard, masculine, gritty.

Tyce thought of Sage's girly loft. She was expensive gems and delicate designs. She was cream couches and soft beds, the wrought iron frame surrounding the bed dotted with tulle and fairy lights. She was expensive; he was functional.

"I'm working on a couple of pieces that I'll be able to sell in a month or two. I want to pay for the baby, your medical expenses to have the baby, for whatever you or the baby needs." He held up his hand. Tyce knew that he could never compete with her wealth. It was stupid to try but he wanted to be able to, at the very least, provide the best for her and his baby. "I know that you can pay for it without my help but...I just want to, okay?"

Sage nodded, her expression inscrutable. "Okay, we'll work it out." Sage sent him an uncertain smile. "So...are we good?"

They were, very good indeed. In fact, he was starting to feel more than good, he felt fan-friggin-tastic. Tyce felt like they'd ripped down a couple of barriers between them, that their fights had flattened some obstacles between them. Or he could be feeling light-headed because he couldn't stop looking at her, drinking her in. Demanding, a little crazy, warm, generous, funny, she was everything he'd ever wanted.

Tyce battled to get his brain to function properly. He knew that he should say something. She was trying, very earnestly, to make amends but all he wanted to do was to blurt out that he thought that they'd turned a corner, they might, maybe, have a shot at...something. Something bigger and brighter than this, whatever this was.

Tyce felt the burn below his rib cage as that thought lodged in his brain. Terror, his childhood companion, drifted into his head, accompanied by doubt, another old ally.

Would he ever be able to fight off both long enough to be with her, to be the man she needed? Deepening his relationship with Sage meant losing his freedom but, at the same time, he couldn't imagine a life without her in it.

He felt dizzy, confused, utterly at sea.

Too much, too soon, Tyce told himself. *You're tired and played out. Think about commitment and monogamy and forever and what you want from her when you aren't punch-drunk with tiredness and overwhelmed by emotion. In the morning you might decide otherwise. This might be an overreaction, a figment of your imagination.*

Take a breath and calm the hell down.

Tyce pushed his hands into the front pockets of his jeans and found his voice. "Want some coffee? I have decaf."

Sage nodded and followed him to the small galley kitchen that ran along the back wall of the apartment. There was also a sitting and dining area and two en suite bedrooms tucked into this corner of the warehouse. A steel-and-wood gangway running above his workshop and home gym linked the apartment to his painting studio. Tyce knew that Sage, who was intensely interested in art, would ask for a tour but his studio, with all the sketches and portraits of her, would be firmly off-limits.

If she saw the many sketches of her she'd definitely think he was a psycho and go running for the hills.

Sage looked up at the pipes running across the ceiling and the massive wooden beams that contrasted with the redbrick walls. Her eyes focused on a massive wooden propeller he'd hung on the far wall and her lips quirked. "I love this… This is you. This is your space. Masculine and minimalistic."

And so very different from her light-filled, pink-tinged, feminine space. If they ever ended up living together, how would they...

Whoa there, cowboy, cool your jets. You decided not to go there, remember? You were going to wait until your brain was functioning properly before you made any life-changing, crazy-ass decisions.

Take a breath, dude. And another...

He focused on making coffee, decaf, of course, then realized he needed something a lot stronger than coffee. He poured a mug for Sage, then reached for a bottle of whiskey and dropped a healthy amount into a glass. Sipping, he felt the burn in his throat, the warmth in his stomach, and his heart slowed down, his lungs opening to allow more air to flow inside. Yeah, that was more like it.

Sage looked around, her eyebrows raised. "So, where's your studio? Where do you paint?"

He'd known she'd ask and instead of blowing her off, as he'd intended to do, he gestured to the door in the corner of the loft. "It's on the other side of the building. Through that door is a catwalk that takes you there."

Sage's eyes lit up. "Can I see it?"

He wanted to say no but he'd just told her that they needed to be honest with each other. Nodding, he walked across the room to open the door onto the gangway. Taking Sage's mug from her, he held her coffee and his whiskey and gestured for her to step out. Sage stepped onto the narrow walkway and looked down at his workbenches and equipment below. He'd just started a new sculpture and pieces of half-bent steel and wood lay scattered across the concrete floor. "What's that going to be?"

Tyce shrugged. "Not sure yet. I'm still waiting for it to make sense."

Sage nodded. Because she was an artist herself, he didn't need to explain the creative process to her, that he was following his instincts, trusting that it would all work out in the end.

"God, it's cold up here," Sage said, wrapping her arms around herself.

"The warehouse is a bitch to heat but I'm normally doing some sort of physical activity down there, either working on a sculpture or working out, so I don't notice it much. The studio is heated."

They'd reached the door that led to his most private space and Tyce took a deep breath as Sage opened the door. "The light switch is on the left."

Sage flipped the switch and light filled the messy room. Tyce handed Sage her mug, took a sip of his whiskey and wondered what she—the first person to step into this space—thought. He looked around, trying to see the familiar setting through new eyes. The windows were incredible, leaded panes letting in every bit of light and shelves held paints and brushes and trowels. Blank canvases were stacked against one wall and there was a half-finished, shades-of-blue abstract taking up the space opposite. Sage looked at the oil for a long time, sipping her coffee before glancing down at the stack of canvases facing the wall. Ah, crap. Well, what had he thought would happen?

"May I?"

Tyce nodded and she immediately sank to the floor, placing the mug by her knee and flipping the first canvas around. He squinted at the charcoal-and-ink sketch and let out a sigh of relief; it was a portrait of Lachlyn, her nose buried in a book. Sage said nothing and turned another canvas around and Tyce sucked in his breath. His mother was lying on the floor next to her bed, her knees pulled up, her eyes vacant.

"She looks a little like Lachlyn... Is this your mom?" Sage asked, glancing up.

Tyce nodded. "Yeah, as I mentioned, she suffered from chronic depression. She'd stay like that for days."

Sage thankfully didn't comment. She just flipped through the portraits, wrinkling her nose when she came across the one of her working at her bench. She looked at the date and lifted her eyes to his, her eyebrows raised. Tyce felt his cheeks warm. "I saw a photo of you in a magazine. I decided to copy it."

Still no comment. Tyce felt ants crawling up his skin as she flipped through the portraits, many of which were of her. After examining the last one, she rested her forearms on her knees.

He saw the anger in her eyes when all that blue slammed into his. "Why the hell have you never exhibited these? They are so good, Tyce, possibly even better than your sculptures and your oils. They are emotional and, sometimes, hard to look at but so damn real!"

Tyce ran a finger along the edge of his ragged sweatshirt, trying to keep up. "I can't do it," he admitted.

"Why on earth not?" Sage cried. "They are fantastic. The emotion jumps off the canvas."

His feelings about her, about them, were a tangled mess but she was still the mother of his child and she deserved to know the truth. The entire truth. Tyce paced the area in front of the oil painting, his fingers holding the glass tumbler in a tight grip. "I discovered that I could sell my portraits when I was thirteen or so. I'd take my sketch pad to Central Park and sketch people who passed by. I'd shove the drawing under their nose and they'd pay me… I still don't know if they paid because they thought the work was good or because they felt sorry for the too-thin kid in old clothes."

Sage quietly sipped of her coffee, her silence encouraging him to continue.

"I did that for a few years. I finished high school and was offered a scholarship to art school but I had to work and the only job I could find was in construction. To make some extra cash, I agreed to pose naked for an art class comprised mostly of women wanting to dabble in art."

Sage just lifted one arched eyebrow higher, looking unaffected. Her shoulders lifted in a tiny *So?*

"I used to draw portraits of the women, which they'd buy. Then they'd take me home and they'd pose naked, telling me that the portrait was for their husband or their lover."

"And you'd end up sleeping with them," Sage said, her tone utterly prosaic.

Tyce rubbed the back of his neck. "I sold many portraits and I slept with quite a few women."

Sage tipped her head to the side and just looked at him. "So?" When he sent her a puzzled look, she continued. "I'm sorry but I'm trying to find the link between you sleeping with someone and why you won't sell your portraits."

Tyce couldn't understand why she was being obtuse. "I slept with them, Sage!"

"You were nineteen and you would've slept with a gorilla if it wore lipstick," Sage replied, impatient. Then the confusion cleared from her eyes. "Oh... wait, I get it. You don't know whether they used the sketches as an excuse to pay you for sex."

Nailed it, Tyce thought morosely, turning away from her.

Tyce heard Sage stand up, heard the sound of her mug hitting the surface of his desk and then felt her hand on his back. He waited for her words, his heart bouncing off his rib cage. "You don't actually know how good you are, do you? That's why you don't attend your own exhibitions, why you don't do interviews... You don't think that you are worth the accolades, the money."

Tyce whirled around and pointed at the oil. "I did that oil in half a day, Sage! I slapped some paint on a canvas, I didn't even think about it and idiots will pay me a quarter mil for it, maybe a whole lot more. The sculptures take more work but nothing that's worth the price tags the galleries put on my pieces. My portraits, they mean something, but yeah, every time I think of selling one, exhibiting one, I feel that I am that confused kid again, trying to keep his head above water, not sure whether he was being pitied or paid for being a stud."

He sucked in a breath and continued. "Art…art was where I retreated to when my mom wouldn't talk, wouldn't move for days on end. It was the place I could hide out in, pretend everything was okay. I used to lose time sketching and drawing. It was the place where I fell into that creative zone where nothing could touch me."

"Are you not going there anymore?" Sage gestured to the oil. "Because this tells me that you are…"

"It's just so damn easy, Sage."

Sage placed her hands on his chest and tipped her lovely face back to look at him, her eyes full of warmth… Love? Affection? "Tyce, you've had a hard life. You've looked after your mother, your sister and you sacrificed so damn much for them, your scholarship, your wealth to buy the Ballantyne shares, your youth. Aren't you allowed to have one thing in your life that's easy? Could this not be life giving you a break?"

Tyce dropped his forehead so that it met hers, hauling in big breaths of much-needed air. Could she be right? Could he finally accept that not everything had to be a fight, a battle to be won?

"You're so talented, Tyce, the most amazing artist I know."

"You're biased." Tyce rumbled the words, so badly
wanting to believe her.

Sage stepped back and looked at him. "Do you
remember when you painted the *Tired Ballerina*?"

The painting in her loft. God, he didn't but it was
early on in his career.

"It was nine years ago and I've always been ob-
sessed about ballet and wished I had the talent to be
a professional dancer. I saw that painting and I fell in
love with it. I was nineteen, twenty? I begged Connor to buy it for me but he wouldn't. When I turned
twenty-one Connor released some money into my
trust fund and I tracked down the owner and I paid
him three times what he originally paid. I hadn't
met you yet but I wanted that painting more than I
wanted to breathe."

Touched, Tyce opened his mouth to speak but she
held up her hand to stop him from saying anything.
"I persuaded my siblings to buy Jaeger one of your
sculptures for a birthday present, and Connor, at my
insistence, bought another three of your paintings for
his private collection. One is on the main wall of the
reception area of Ballantyne International. Connor
said that, while he'd never liked the *Tired Ballerina*,
he loved your new work. He said that you were going
to be one of the best and one of the most influential
artists of the twenty-first century and... Guess what?
You are. You are worth every cent you are paid. If

you don't believe one word I've ever said, please, please, believe that."

Tyce closed his eyes, not wanting her to see the emotion there and he dug his fingers into her skin, hoping that she wouldn't feel the trembling in his hands. He felt both tired and rejuvenated, wiped out and energized.

And God, free. Sage's words made him feel empowered, unrestricted. She made him feel like he could take on the world single-handed and win. He wanted to tell her how much what she'd said meant to him, how life-changing it was, but the words stuck in his throat. He ducked his head and hoped that he could convey what he was trying to say with his mouth, his hands, by worshipping her body.

But Sage was way ahead of him. She stood on her toes and placed her lips on his, her tongue tracing the seam of his lips, demanding that he open up. He whispered a *Hell, yeah* and she slid her tongue into his and she dialed up the temperature, demanding his response. Tyce yanked her to him, his hands looking for bare skin. He was still pulling her shirt out of her jeans when Sage's hand slid under his sweatshirt and her fingers tap-danced their way across his abs, her thumb swiping the space between his belly button and the low band of his jeans. His stomach muscles contracted and she groaned her approval and her kisses turned wild.

Then Sage's hands attacked the button on his jeans. Who was this woman taking control, whose hand was sliding underneath his underwear to encircle him? She'd been timid, sometimes shy about telling him what turned her on but today she knew exactly what she wanted. Tyce felt blood pump into his erection and he turned rock hard in her hand.

Sage gave another throaty murmur of approval and she wrenched her mouth from his and stepped back to pull his shirt up and over his head. As soon as his chest was bare she slapped her open mouth against his sternum, her tongue tracing a fiery path down his body.

Holy crap, she couldn't possibly be thinking of...

He'd pleasured her like this before but he knew that she wasn't comfortable, yet, to reciprocate. He'd spent many, many nights imagining Sage doing exactly this but his imagination, which was powerful, had nothing on this. Her tongue flicked over his abs and he groaned and reached back to grab the edge of a shelf, convinced that his knees were about to buckle.

Sage pushed his jeans down his legs and worked her fingers under the band of his underwear. Cool air touched his straining erection and her fiery mouth on his skin was a complete contrast. He didn't know if he could handle this: his fantasies had fallen well short of how she made him feel. In his dreams, his heart never felt like it was about to beat through his chest, like he didn't have a single spark of brain-power left, that the whole world was reduced to her mouth on him.

He couldn't do it... It was too much. Then Sage

took him inside her mouth, and his brain, that teeny tiny organ, shut down completely.

Tyce gripped the counter and tipped his head back, thinking that if he watched her, he'd lose it completely. His chest heaved and beads of sweat popped on his skin. This, Sage, being loved by her, was all his fantasies and wishes and hopes and dreams coming true.

Oh, it wasn't just about the sex—which was terrifyingly fantastic—but all of this. She was in his studio and she'd said everything he most needed to hear about his art, had placed his past actions into perspective, had opened up a new world to him. He wanted this, all of it. He wanted her in his life, to be a big part of hers, he wanted to raise their baby together. That much he knew… There would be no thinking about this in the morning.

He needed her. He always had.

Tyce gripped her shoulders, pulled her up and slapped his mouth on hers. In between hot and heavy kisses, they managed to pull their clothes off, scattering them across his paint-splattered floor. When they were both naked, Tyce locked his arms beneath her bottom and lifted her up, sighing when her slim legs encircled his waist. Unable to wait, he pushed her down and he slid into her, wet and warm and wonderful.

Sage gasped and Tyce saw stars behind his eyes. Not convinced that his knees weren't about to buckle, he rested her against his oil painting, and Sage's head fell back. Tyce stopped and looked at her, eyes closed, long hairs falling through the still-wet paint of his creation, her milky shoulders against the various shades of blue.

Knowing that he couldn't hold on for much longer, Tyce commanded Sage to open her eyes. When she did, he sighed and fell a little deeper in love. "I want to watch your eyes as you come. But do it soon, please?"

Sage pressed down, her butt sliding down the canvas, and he sunk even farther into her. She gasped, yelled and contracted around him and he was lost.

Then he spun away into a vortex of a million shades of blue.

The next morning, Tyce walked Sage to the taxi and she noticed the amusement in his eyes as he pulled a cap over her head.

"What?" she mock demanded, thinking that he looked, if it was possible, ten times sexier than he had last night. He had rings around his eyes, so did she since they hadn't spent much time sleeping, but the shadows in his eyes were gone.

"I was just thinking about the streaks of French ultramarine on your butt," he told her, laughter rolling through his expression.

Sage frowned at him. "I'm more upset that you destroyed your painting than I am about some oil paint on my ass."

Last night, when they came up for air and were marginally functional, Sage felt the wet paint on her bottom and had whirled around to look at the painting, which now sported a perfect imprint of her butt cheeks. Instead of being upset about his ruined painting, Tyce had cried with laughter.

"I'll do something with it," Tyce told her, lifting his hands to cradle her face. "Maybe. Or I might just keep it as a reminder of the best sex of my life. And the best conversation."

Sage smiled and curled her gloved hands around his strong wrists. "Just remember that I think you are fabulous."

Tyce lifted one arrogant eyebrow but she saw the hint of uncertainty in his eyes. "A fabulous artist?"

"Just all round fabulous."

Tyce smiled, lowered his mouth to hers and gently kissed it. His mouth held a hint of passion but it went deeper than that; she could taste his promises, the suggestion of a future together. The hope that this time they could make it work, that they could be better and braver.

"What's your plan of action for the day?" Tyce asked her when he lifted his mouth from hers.

"Um… I have a client meeting at Ballantyne's and then I'm heading home as I have to finish the Saudi princess's ring." Sage glanced at the taxi driver. He wasn't looking impatient yet so she had a minute or two. "And your plans?"

"When you fell asleep, I started to think about all the work I'm dying to do so I might hole up here and just…work. Fall into that zone."

Sage smiled, immediately understanding what he was trying to say. "So, if you don't answer my calls or respond to my texts I mustn't panic?"

"That okay with you?"

Sage smiled and nodded. "Very okay. Let me know when you come up for air. But it had better be before Thursday morning as we have a ten o'clock appointment with Dr. Charles, the obstetrician."

"Day after tomorrow at ten. No problem," Tyce told her. "I'm pretty sure that my need to have you again will bring me back to the land of the living way before then."

Sage stood on her toes to slant her mouth over his in a hot, openmouthed kiss. "Can't wait. Have fun."

Tyce opened the passenger door to the taxi and when she was seated, he bent down to kiss her again. His fabulous eyes were full of mischief when he pulled back. "Oh, and maybe I should tell you that you have blue streaks running through the back of your hair."

He slammed the door shut but Sage could still hear his laughter. She pushed her hat off her head and pulled a hank of hair in front of her face. Lifting her eyes upward, she immediately noticed the strands of French ultramarine.

Dammit! She spun around to look out through the window at Tyce and saw that he was looking down, his eyes on the screen of his phone.

Ten seconds later her phone buzzed with an incoming text.

Want to come back? I'm have this idea of tossing paint onto a canvas and rolling around in it with you. It would be a piece for my very private collection.

Sage smiled, shuddered with longing and flipped another look over her shoulder but Tyce had gone back into his building.

So tempted, Sage typed back, But I doubt the Saudi princess, or my boss brother, would understand me blowing off a meeting with one of our biggest clients to play with paint. Rain check?

Eleven

"Do you want to get some coffee?" Tyce asked Lachlyn as they left the small, warm studio and stepped into the icy wind barreling down the street. Lachlyn had asked him to meet her at a new gallery she'd discovered, thinking that he'd enjoy the eclectic pieces sourced from all over the world. He had.

"Sure." Lachlyn looked around. "There's a coffee shop at the end of the block."

"Sage's apartment is around the corner. She's at a meeting at Ballantyne HQ but her coffee is fantastic."

Lachlyn nodded her agreement and they started walking in the direction of Sage's apartment. "How is Sage?" she asked.

"Fine. Why do you ask?"

"Oh, because when you told me you were moving

in with her after her accident, you said it would just be for a couple of days. It's been a couple of weeks and you're still there. Did she crack her spine or is her arm paralyzed?"

Tyce narrowed her eyes at his sister. "Smart-ass."

But it was fair question. Why was he still living with Sage? Every day he made the trek to Brooklyn, worked in his studio and at night he made his way back to SoHo. It was because making love with Sage was like a Class A drug and he was hooked. He couldn't imagine a day without her in it, not waking up next to her, exploring her body every night. God, that sounded like he was...

No, don't say it, don't think it. His need to be with her had nothing to do with the L-word, or a future they could spend together, a life they could make. He was still the reserved, taciturn, need-to-be-alone artist he always was.

Except that his actions, every damned day, contradicted his words. *Crap.*

"So, what did you think of The Den?" he asked in a deliberate attempt to change the subject. They hadn't had any time to talk about her meeting the Ballantynes and how she felt about her new family. Talking about The Den, and Lachlyn's extensive tour of the house with Jo, Linc's mother, was his way of easing into that conversation.

"Oh, Tyce...it's definitely the most amazing house I've ever seen." Lachlyn shoved her gloved hand into the crook of his elbow and snuggled in. "There is a Picasso hanging in a small sitting room, Lalique glassware everywhere and, I swear, what I thought might be a Fabergé egg."

Remotely possible but not likely, Tyce thought.

"You only saw the one lounge and the formal dining room but Linc and Tate mostly use a massive room that's as normal as any I've seen. There were toys on the floor, drawings on the fridge. Okay, admittedly, most people don't have purple crayons squished into Persian carpets but I liked that room. I could see that Tate and Linc *lived* there."

Lachlyn continued her description of the iconic brownstone occupied by generations of Ballantynes and he let her ramble because he was interested in the house Sage grew up in. His ears pricked up at the mention of Linc's state-of-the-art gym and climate-controlled wine cellar in the basement.

"And Sage?" Tyce asked, his heart picking up speed. "What did you think of her?"

Sage and Lachlyn were the two women who were going to be in his life for a long, long time. It was important that they liked each other. And they were also now part of the same family. That was important too.

"She's a little prickly." His sister frowned. "Maybe that's not the right word... Scared? Vulnerable?"

"But do you *like* her?" Tyce persisted.

"Yes, I suppose I do." Lachlyn frowned again. "We were supposed to have dinner this week but she postponed. I've sent her a couple of texts trying to reschedule but she's booked up at the moment."

Tyce frowned at the note of hurt he heard in Lachlyn's voice. Trying to reassure her, he put his arm around her shoulder and hugged her close. "I have heard many mutterings of a picky Saudi princess who can't make up her damn mind."

They turned the corner onto Sage's block and, like a homing beacon, Tyce's eyes were drawn to a slim figure at the end of the street, wearing black pants tucked into black boots, and a scarlet coat. Sage was looking down at her phone and wasn't paying attention to her surroundings.

Tyce nudged Lachlyn. "Sage is home early—her meeting must have been rescheduled. Let's catch up with her."

Lachlyn looked anxious. "Let me give her a heads-up, tell her that I'm here."

"Nah, let's just go," Tyce insisted. "It's too cold to hang around."

Lachlyn shook her head and pulled out her phone, pressing buttons. Tyce looked down, saw that her phone was dialing Sage's number and looked across the road. He watched Sage look down at her phone and when she grimaced, he knew that she had read the caller ID. Instead of answering Lachlyn's call, she shoved her phone back into her coat pocket.

His temper bubbled and when he clocked Lachlyn's miserable expression, it burned a hole in his stomach. His sister blinked away her tears and tried to smile. "Yeah, so I guess it's me and not work that's the problem."

"Lach—" Tyce said, at a loss for what to say. He looked down into her bewildered face and, in that moment, his baby sister was wearing the exact ex-

pression that was a feature of her childhood spent
with their mother.

*I love you—what's wrong with me that you can't
love me back? Do I make you sad? Am I the problem?*

Lachlyn reached up to kiss his cheek. "It's okay,
Tyce. Maybe she's not ready for me." Lachlyn pat-
ted his arm. "I'll talk to you later, okay?"

Tyce watched Lachlyn walk away, anger and disappointment rolling through him. He looked across the
street, all his anger directed at Sage, who was walking, head down, toward the front door of her place.
Tyce took his own phone and dialed her number...

Sage looked down at her phone and saw Tyce's
name flash on her screen. Lifting the phone to her
ear, she stopped and turned toward the side of the
building, putting her back to the wind. "Hi."

"Hey." Tyce's voice sounded funny but Sage
thought that it could just be the wind playing tricks
with her ears.

"I'm with Lachlyn and I thought that we could
come to the apartment for coffee. Are you going to
be home soon?"

Yeah, he definitely sounded weird. Almost angry,
Sage thought. Sage rubbed the back of her neck, trying to massage the tension away. Her princess had arrived ten minutes late for their meeting and stormed
out in a huff after another five, declaring that Sage's
designs were all rubbish and plebeian and that she
hated every one.

She felt battered and tired and all she wanted was

to climb into a hot bath and to go to bed early. She
didn't want to talk to anyone, not even Tyce, tonight.
She felt like she hadn't had a moment alone for the
month and all she wanted was an empty apartment
and some quiet.

"Sage? Are you there?"

"I'm still at work." The lie ran smoothly off her
tongue even as it burned a hole in her stomach. But
if she told him the truth, then he'd demand to know
why she needed time alone, what was bugging her,
why she was avoiding him and his sister. She just
didn't have the energy to deal with any of it.

"I'm going to be working late so—" she hesitated
"—maybe you should stay at your place tonight?"

"Okay then."

Sage looked down at her dead phone and winced.
God, she hated lying and wished she hadn't. She
should've just told him that she needed some time
alone; of everyone she knew, Tyce was the person
most likely to understand that. And he was a big boy;
if he asked what was wrong and she said that she
didn't feel like talking, he'd understand. There was
no need to lie...yet she'd done it. Sage felt acid coat
her throat, feeling thoroughly ashamed of herself.

She'd have to confess the lie and that wasn't going
to be fun.

But she was a big girl and she'd done the crime,
so she'd take the consequences.

Sage looked down at her screen and saw the
"missed" call she'd ignored from Lachlyn and re-

morse swamped her. And she felt guilty for blowing their plans, for using work as an excuse to avoid her.

Sage sucked in some cold air thinking that it was bad timing, that she did need to get on top of work; she didn't really have the time to start a new relationship. With Tyce living with her and taking up her time at night and the tiredness from the pregnancy hormones, and the horrible weather…

And the famine in the Sudan and the bomb blast in Pakistan and the phase of the moon…

God, she was just one crazy, twisted knot of excuses.

The truth was that she was scared. No, terrified. Scared of what she felt for Tyce, scared of what she could feel for Lachlyn. Scared of being hurt, left alone, lost.

But, most of all, she was scared to live. To love.

Sage wrapped her arms around her waist as she walked the last yards to her building. A series of pictures flashed into her head and they were of the last vacation she'd spent with her parents. They'd flown to Hawaii and she remembered they'd all taken surfing lessons. Her brothers had picked up the skill immediately but she and her dad had struggled to find their balance. On the cinema screen in her head, her mom, who was a Californian girl, was skimming down what looked like, to her, a monstrous wave. Her dark hair was flying, she was whooping like a maniac and she had the most enormous smile on her face.

Her dad had looked at her and grinned. "That's your mom, Sagie. Wild and free, so in love with life."

Sage wiped a tear off her face and thought that she might look like her mom but she wasn't anything like her. She was cautious and closed off and a slave to her fears. Yes, she'd experienced incredible personal loss but she'd survived it and if it happened again, she would survive that too. Hearts might get dinged and broken but they didn't actually kill you.

She could, Sage realized, spend the rest of her life in a cage where it was safe and, yeah, boring, or she could break out of jail and start to explore her world. She was young, rich and reasonably smart; she could have a wonderful life if she found a little bit of her mom's courage, her bold spirit.

Someday, not today, she would have to try. She owed that to the memory of her parents, to Connor...

"So, working late, huh?"

Sage let out a low scream as Tyce appeared beside her, a yard from the steps leading up to the front door. Sage slapped her hand against her heart as she caught her breath. "Dammit, Tyce! I hate it when you do that!"

"Yeah?" Tyce's eyes were as hard and cold as frozen coal. "Coincidentally, I hate it when you lie to me."

Oh, crap, she was so busted. Sage scratched her forehead, looking for the right words. Tyce didn't give her a chance. "So, who were you blowing off? Me? Lachlyn? Both of us?"

Sage shoved her shaking hands into the pockets

of her coat. Before she could reply, her phone rang and she pulled it out. Blessing Linc for the interruption since it gave her a little time to construct a decent apology, she answered his call. Linc was hoping for a date night with Tate and was wondering if she could babysit Shaw and Ellie.

"Sorry, Linc, not tonight. I'm exhausted and I have a headache and all I want to do is climb into a hot bath and go to bed early." Sage forced herself to look at Tyce, sighing at his hard expression. This is what she should've said to him instead of that stupid lie. "I just need some time alone."

"No worries, I'll ask Beck and Cady. Later."

Sage disconnected the call and before she could speak, Tyce did. "So, you need some space, huh? No problem." Tyce started to walk away but Sage caught his sleeve and tugged, her actions asking him to stay. Suddenly she didn't want to be alone. She just wanted to step into his arms, allow his strength and solidity to suck the tension from her. In his arms, she realized, was the place she felt safest.

"Tyce—"

Tyce's snapped-out swear was the perfect accompaniment to his pissed-off scowl. "I am so mad at you, Sage. You lied to me and that's a pretty big deal to me. I don't deal in lies. But worse than that, you hurt my sister. I'm not sure what games you are playing, but she wants to get to know you, to be your friend, that's all she's asking." Tyce pointed to a spot down and across the street. "We saw you walking. Lachlyn called you and you pulled a face when you saw her name on your phone. That was strike one. You let her call ring out and Lachlyn watched you do it. Strike two."

Sage felt like he'd stabbed her in the heart. Ah, no, damn, no.

"She walked away from me, crying. Then you freaking lied to me? Strike three, Sage."

"You set me up!" Sage retorted. "You wanted to see what I would do, say."

"That's your defense?" Tyce gripped her arms in his big hands, bending down so that his face was level with hers. "Bad move, Ballantyne. Lachlyn and I spent our childhoods with a mother who didn't love us enough to want to get better, who didn't want us around and gave us no attention. She certainly had no interest in getting to know us, on any level. It was far more fun being a chronic depressive. My point is, we know when we're not wanted."

His voice, so calm and so controlled, cut through her. Sage felt hot tears running down her cheeks. "Tyce, I'm sorry. I didn't mean to make either of you feel like that."

Tyce dropped his hands, held them up and stepped away. "As I said… You want space? Take as much as you need."

Sage held her fist to her mouth as she watched Tyce stride away. She called out to him in the vain hope that he would turn around and come back. Tyce just broke into a jog, leaving her standing in the icy wind.

Ashamed and annoyed at herself, and so very embarrassed, Sage looked up at her building and considered going up. She could take that bath and try for an early night but she knew that the chances of her sleeping were minimal at best. She was exhausted but sleep would be elusive unless she found Tyce and apologized. Sage thought about using her cell phone to call him but that would be too easy, the cowardly way out. She needed to look him in the eye and take her medicine like the big girl she now was.

Where would he have gone on a cold winter's night? To the apartment in Chelsea or the studio in Brooklyn? He'd go to where his art was, Sage decided. If he was half as frustrated as she was, then he'd try to lose himself in his work, to fall into that space where pesky problems and annoying people faded away.

But before she went to Tyce, she had to mend a blown-up fence. Sage pulled out her phone. She held her breath, knowing that the chance of her call being answered was slim to none.

"Hello?"

"Lach?" Sage heard her voice break as she used Tyce's pet name for his sister. "I've really messed up. Firstly, I'm sorry that I ignored your call—I'm not very good at letting people in and I got scared. I'm really, really sorry."

"Okay," Lachlyn replied, her tone cautious.

"You are so like Connor, Lachlyn. It's taking some time to get used to."

"I can't help that," Lachlyn said, her voice cool.

"I know," Sage replied. "Just give me some time, please? I'm feeling a little overwhelmed."

"So am I, Sage."

God, she'd never considered the situation from Lachlyn's point of view, she'd never thought about how hard it had to be to step into a family and wonder if they'd like her, even love her. Sage had been so selfish, so caught up in her own drama.

These Latimores certainly had a way of making her see herself clearly.

"I can forgive you for hurting me, Sage, but I will never forgive you if you hurt Tyce. If you ask me to pick a side between you and your brothers, or Tyce, I will, always, always pick Tyce. Do not doubt that."

Sage appreciated the sentiment and she respected Lachlyn's loyalty to her brother.

"I'm going to head to his studio to apologize."

"That's not a good idea and he won't appreciate it. Give him some time and space to deal with his anger," Lachlyn suggested.

"Okay." Sage rubbed the back of her neck. "I am sorry for earlier, Lachlyn. And I need you to know that it's not my intention to hurt Tyce."

"Really?" Lachlyn sounded skeptical. "For someone who is acting unintentionally, you're doing a damn fine job of doing just that."

The next evening, Sage stood in the doorway of the sitting room of The Den holding Ellie. She looked across the space to the Ballantyne women. Piper and Cady sat on the Persian carpet on either side of Amy, and Tate sat on the big leather couch close to them. Each of them held a book containing fabric swatches but only Amy was flipping through hers and cursing like a sailor. There were four books of open fabric samples on the carpet in front of her and another five on the coffee table. From her position in the doorway, Sage could only see minuscule differences in the shades of cream.

Sage rubbed her cheek against Ellie's curls and cuddled the little girl closer. Linc had bundled her into her arms as soon as she stepped into The Den, telling her that Shaw had accidentally emptied an entire bottle of bath bubbles into his bath.

Accidentally-on-purpose, Sage was sure.

"What are you doing?" Sage asked the women.

Four heads swiveled around and Tate crossed the room to her, giving her, and Ellie, a warm hug. Ellie deserted Sage by tumbling into her mom's arms.

Sage greeted everyone and gestured to the books. "What are you trying to decide? Can I help?"

"The exact shade of cream for the reception tablecloths."

Behind Amy, Cady rolled her eyes, and Sage hid her smile. There had been murmurs of Amy turning into Bridezilla but only when they were very, very sure that Amy wasn't around. Amy, as Linc and Beck's PA, was the power behind the Ballantyne throne.

"Jules told me that I am driving her mad with the wedding arrangements and she's threatening to kidnap me and take me to Vegas." Amy pushed out her bottom lip. "I just want it to be perfect."

Sage bent down and gave her a hug. "You're overthinking it, honey. Choose one—they are all pretty much the same."

Amy glared at the books. "I will. After I look through the books on the floor once more. How are you?"

Sage shrugged, thinking that there was no point in lying. "Horrible." Sage plopped down into the corner of the couch and rubbed the back of her neck. "I really messed up. Again."

Four sets of sympathetic eyes rested on her face and, for the first time ever, the words tumbled out of her as she explained what a complete idiot she'd been and how she'd hurt Lachlyn. And Tyce.

"I apologized to Lachlyn and I've tried to call Tyce, repeatedly, but he's ignoring me," Sage said.

She shoved her hands into her hair and saw the sympathetic faces. She lifted up her hand. "Don't feel too sorry for me, guys—this was all my fault. I knew that if I allowed myself to get close that I'd get hurt."

Sage stared at the books of fabric swatches, her eyes wet with tears. "I love him. I do. I think I always have but as soon as he gets too close, I push him away."

Tate sank to the floor next to her legs and rested her temple against Sage's knee. "Oh, honey. What are you going to do?"

Sage shrugged. Since this was the first time she'd frankly and openly admitted that she loved Tyce, to herself as well as to her family, she hadn't given the next step much thought. "I don't know. I know I need to apologize but I can't do that unless I speak to him. And I don't know if I can do the whole sleeping-together-without-love thing anymore. I want to tell him that I love him but I think that he might run. Fast and hard." Sage placed a hand on her stomach. "And, man, that will hurt like a bitch and you guys know how hard I work to avoid being hurt."

"So you love him?" Tate asked.

Sage nodded. "Yes, I love him." Of that much she was sure. "I always have."

"So do it," Tate said, her voice firm.

Sage frowned. "Sorry, what?"

"So you're scared, so he might run. Do it anyway," Tate said, resting her hand on Sage's thigh. "We think that we have to get rid of the fear first when, actually, what we have to do is act first. Only then does the fear go away."

Cady nodded. "The only way to stop being afraid of loving someone is to love them."

Sage stared at her flat biker boots. "But what if he leaves?" she quietly asked. "Or dies?"

"Then he leaves or dies," Piper said. She climbed to her feet and, moving behind her, leaned over and wrapped her arms around Sage's waist, her chin on her shoulder. "We can't be responsible for, or try to control, what other people do, baby. We only have control over our actions. We can only worry about what we can control."

Sage hugged Piper's arms to her, her eyes filling

with tears. This was what a support base felt like,
what belonging to a tribe of strong women felt like.
These were the Ballantyne women—Sage had always thought that Amy should change her name to
Ballantyne and be done with it—and they were a
unit. And, her blurry eyes focused on her niece, who
was sitting in Tate's lap, they were raising another
generation of strong Ballantyne women.

Their wise counsel made sense and she was grateful for it. She wasn't sure if she'd take their advice
but she'd certainly think about it. She'd think about
it a lot.

"Wine!" Amy said, standing up. "I know that Linc
recently bought a case of Domaine de la Romanée-
Conti. He won't miss a bottle, or three."

Tate groaned. "He'll kill us, Ames. It's one of the
most expensive wines in the world."

"Pfft." Amy waved her concerns away.

"Touch my wine and you're fired," Linc said,
striding into the room. He walked into the center
of the carpet, dropped a kiss on his wife's head and
grinned when his daughter held up her arms, her face
splitting into a huge smile at the sight of her dad.

Sage fought tears and tried not to think of her
baby looking at Tyce like that. She owed it to their
child, she owed it to herself, to tell Tyce how she
felt, to express what she wanted. If she didn't, she'd
regret it for the rest of her life.

She needed to be brave because if she wasn't,
how would she teach her child to be courageous, to
take a chance?

Yes, it was scary; yes, terror was congealing her blood but Tyce was worth a little fear.

Sage just stared at the carpet—Was that a purple crayon buried in the threads?—as determination pushed fear into a corner, holding it at bay. She could do this. She would do this.

Sage stood up, smiled and headed for the door. The last thing she heard as she bolted out was Tate's cheerful statement. "That's our girl. Ames, the case of wine is still in the hallway—neither Linc or I have had a minute to take it down to the cellar. Go grab a bottle. Or three."

Twelve

We really need to talk.

Tyce looked at his phone and sighed. Yeah, they did. *Where are you?*

Tyce waited for her reply message to appear on his screen. Sage was at The Den. Of course she was; when her world fell apart she had a place, people to run to. He didn't. Neither did Lachlyn.

I can come to you. Are you at your studio?

Tyce shook his head, a futile gesture since Sage couldn't see it.

Just finished dinner with my agent. I'll come to you.

Okay. I'll wait.

Tyce stepped off the pavement and raised his arm to hail a taxi, cursing when the cab cruised past him. He jammed his bare hands into the pockets of his leather bomber jacket.

Another yellow cab turned down the street and Tyce held up his hand, thinking he'd lose it if the cab didn't stop. It did and he yanked the door open and climbed inside, tossing the address to the driver. He dropped his temple to the cool window and, staring at the rain-soaked city, he became aware of the headache pounding his temples.

Too much talking, he thought. His argument with Sage left a sour taste in his mouth and a stain on his soul. Every time he felt like they were moving forward, Sage pushed them backward.

Tyce felt the hard knot of tension in his stomach, knowing it was there because he was sure that she was going to call it off, to put them firmly in the friends and co-parent category.

He couldn't blame her because how could they keep taking five steps forward and six backward?

They'd been together for nearly a month and their expiration date was closing in on them. Sage had to be feeling antsy and, like before, she wanted out.

Tyce ordered his heart to pick itself up from the floor. Breaking up wasn't a bad move, Tyce rationalized, because he knew that being alone was so much easier. When he was alone he didn't feel drained. Lonely? Sure. Emotionally exhausted? No.

He hadn't been so at sea since before his mom died, and he'd forgotten what it felt like to *feel*. It wasn't fun. Tyce felt like he was walking along the edge of a precipice, one slip and he'd crash and break. Yeah, he could move on from this fight but there would always be another, and another…

He'd escaped a life of emotional drama; he'd run from relationships because he hated feeling like he was a vessel constantly being emptied and never re-filled.

These fights, dealing with Sage's issues, sucked him dry. His thoughts were a million miles from his art, from his livelihood and he couldn't afford to be distracted. He had a bank account to replenish and he'd need every ounce of energy he had to deal with becoming a dad, being the best father he could.

So when Sage called it quits, he'd kiss her on the cheek and walk away because, dammit, *he was better off alone*. He knew how to be alone. Loneliness didn't scare him; emotion did. When he lived his life alone, he had control, he was in his comfort zone.

Sage, this up-and-down relationship, took him way out of his comfort zone. He'd started to rely on her when he'd only ever relied on himself.

That scared the living hell out of him. What had he been thinking?

Enough of that, Tyce suddenly decided. He couldn't, wouldn't do that anymore.

If she, he, they, called it quits today—and that was going to happen—then they'd have four or five months on their own to get used to the idea of not sleeping together—of not sharing a life together. They'd be able to act like mature adults as they figured out a way to raise their child together.

But he'd always want her...

Don't think about that, dingbat. Don't go there... You have to do this or else you are going to be miserable for the rest of your life.

Okay, more miserable, he clarified.

His decision made—God, it might be the right one but it still sucked—Tyce moved on to problem number two. Before the week was out, their lives—all their lives, his, Sage's, Lachlyn's and the rest of the Ballantynes'—would be turned on their heads. Turned on their heads? Tyce snorted at his choice of words. There was a crap storm coming and there was no hiding from it.

Earlier Lachlyn called and told him that she'd been accosted by a reporter on her way to work and had been subjected to a barrage of questions. Was she Connor's daughter? Did the Ballantynes know? Was she owner of Lach-Ty, the company that'd made bulk purchases of Ballantyne shares? Lachlyn sounded like she was on the verge of tears and Tyce could hear the relentless yapping of the reporter in the background. He'd rapidly changed directions to go to Lachlyn, to see who was harassing her and to try to ascertain how much the reporter actually knew.

The guy knew a lot more than Tyce was comfortable with. When he arrived on Lachlyn's doorstep, Tyce got into his face, demanding to know where he'd stumbled across this information. The young reporter, at least a foot shorter than Tyce but ridiculously confident, refused to divulge his sources. Tyce endured fifteen minutes batting off his pointed questions, hoping for a hint of the source, but he earned nothing more than a headache.

After the reporter left, he spent another hour with Lachlyn, watching her pace her living room and listening to her rambling commentary about the Ballantynes and whether she wanted to become a member of the famous family or not. Of course she did; she liked all of them. She was just rattled by the reporter's verbal attack.

Whether she wanted to or not, Tyce knew that she no longer had a choice. The story was going to break sooner rather than later and all they could do was manage the process. Maybe they should just announce Sage's pregnancy at the same time; it might get lost in the bigger news of a brand-new Ballantyne. If they announced it at a later stage, it would just give this story legs. Damned press, why couldn't they just leave them the hell alone to walk through the chaos of their lives on their own?

Realizing that the taxi had pulled up outside The Den, Tyce paid the cab driver and walked through the gate and up those imposing steps.

This would be the last time, for a while at least, that he'd stand in front of this door, the last time he'd see Sage.

They had to do this, he reminded himself, placing his hand on the door. Because a little hurt now would avoid open heart surgery later.

He didn't need her; he didn't anyone. He never had.

Sage, sitting on a stair halfway up to the next floor, saw Linc open the front door to The Den and looked through the slats down into the hallway and watched Tyce step into her childhood home.

This is it, she thought, do or die.

She knew that if she didn't ask for what she wanted, she had no chance of getting it, that if she didn't step forward she'd always be in the same place.

It was an easy concept to think about but putting those words into action was going to be an act of epic proportions.

Oh, God…she was about to risk her heart, her pride, her damned safety when she told Tyce that she wanted more, needed more… What the hell was she doing? Was she mad?

Do it anyway, a little voice said inside her. *Whether it's mad or not, safe or not, do it anyway.*

Sage stood up and Tyce immediately looked up, frustration and something that might be fear in his eyes. Sage walked down the staircase, her hand resting on her belly, noticing the purple stripes under Tyce's eyes.

Yeah, she hadn't slept much either.

"Hey," Sage said, stopping on the last step, her hand gripping the banister.

"Hey."

"Thanks for coming over."

Tyce jammed his hands into the front pockets of his jeans and shrugged. "Sure."

Sage heard footsteps and looked past Tyce's shoulder. Oh, God, the crew from downstairs were now all in the hall, their faces alight with curiosity. Did they really expect her to spill her soul in front of them? It was a strong possibility.

"We're all heading out," Amy said, holding a book of fabric swatches under her arm.

"Give us five seconds to grab our coats and we'll get out of your way," Piper said, her eyes darting between her face and Tyce.

Tyce waved them into the room. "Hell, come on in," he said. "When have Sage and I ever had a conversation that you lot haven't, in some way, been a part of?"

He sounded blasé but Sage could see the tension in his body, the anger in his eyes.

"That's not fair!" Sage hurled the words at him. She reined in her temper and concentrated on her breathing. If they started a fight now, if they waited for the crew to leave, she'd never say what she needed to.

Ignoring her family, Sage focused on Tyce, moving up to him and placing her hand on his heart. "I'm sorry. I was so completely out of line and I'm asking for your forgiveness."

Tyce pushed an agitated hand through his hair and stepped back, breaking the contact between them. When she didn't speak again, Tyce lifted an eyebrow.

"That it?" he asked and gestured to the door. "If yes, then I'm going to head out because I'm pretty beat."

Sage heard, and ignored, the gasp from her audience. "No, that's not it," Sage said, forcing steel into her spine. Putting her hands behind her back, she twisted her fingers together.

"I can't do this anymore." Sage picked out her words, careful with each one.

Tyce handed her a quick, jerky nod. "Yeah, me neither. Let's just call it quits before this blows up in our faces."

Oh, God, oh, Jesus. Sage placed her hand on her stomach as his words smacked into her. He was breaking up with her?

What the hell?

Sage fought the instinct to back away, to agree with him. It would be so easy to smile, to nod, to agree with his assessment of the situation. To allow him to walk away. But that wasn't what she wanted. She wanted a lover, a partner, someone to live her life with, to share the momentous occasions and the ordinary.

She wanted him in her life on an everyday basis.

Sage shook her head. "I'm sorry you feel that way but that wasn't what I was going to say."

Tyce frowned. "Sorry?"

"I don't want to break up, in fact I'd like us to be together. Permanently."

Tyce just stared at her, shock on his face. Sage didn't know what else to say, how to express her heart, how to ask for what she wanted. Didn't he understand that she was willing to risk her stable, constant life for one filled with a lot of passion, a little uncertainty, risk? Didn't he understand how hard it was for her to be in this position, to love someone so much and be scared of being rejected? Words, pleading, desperate words bubbled in her throat and as they rose they burst apart and all that remained was a bitter taste on her tongue.

But she knew that if she didn't speak them, if she let them die, if she let him walk out that door without expressing them, she'd lose the moment forever.

Tyce took a step back and, operating on instinct, Sage grabbed the open sides of his leather bomber jacket to hold him in place. He started to pry her hands off but she tightened her grip and shook her head.

"All I'm asking you to do is to stand here and listen to me, just for a minute, maybe two. I know you are angry but you need to hear this. You need to hear *me*."

"You've got two minutes and that's it," Tyce growled.

"Okay, I'll keep it short."

Sage pulled in a deep breath and looked for her courage. This was too vital to mess up but her tongue was battling to form the words. Voice croaky, she got the first sentence out. "I love you. I think I fell in love with you the first time I saw you and I've loved nobody else, ever. I want you, I want us. You, me, our baby, a family."

Tyce didn't react and just stood statue still.

"Be my family, Tyce, within this family. Yeah, my brothers are annoying but you can handle them."

Still no response. Sage blew out a breath, dropped her hands and stared down at the floor. "If my love isn't enough, then walk out that door and we'll communicate about the baby through lawyers."

It was an ultimatum but she had to know, she couldn't live with maybes or possibilities. He either loved her or he didn't, he either wanted a life with her or didn't. It was actually a fairly simple choice.

Tyce shook his head. His words, when he finally spoke, felt like splashes of acid on her soul. "It won't work, Sage. I'm sorry."

"Now it's your turn to push me away."

Tyce nodded. "It's easier to be alone... We both know this." Out of the corner of her eye, she saw Tate's hand shoot out to grab Linc's arm as he stepped forward. Really? Did Linc think that he could force Tyce to stay? Feeling shocked and saddened, Sage watched as Tyce opened the front door with a vicious yank. In the open doorway, he stopped abruptly and Sage couldn't help the surge of relief, the rush of hope.

Maybe he'd changed his mind; maybe he was prepared to give them a chance.

Instead of moving toward her, Tyce looked at Linc instead. "You should know that, somehow, certain members of the press have information about Lachlyn, about Lach-Ty and about her connection to Connor. Handle it any way you see fit."

"Tyce—" Linc stepped forward and Tyce shook his head and stepped into the cold, dark night.

Sage stared at the door for a long time before turning back to her family. She tried to smile but she could feel her chin wobbling, the tears sliding down her cheeks. "So," she said, trying for jaunty but failing miserably, "anyone have any idea what I can do about this gaping, bloody hole where my heart used to reside?"

Tyce, standing in his studio, released a violent curse and threw his custom-made palette knife across the room so that it bounced off a wall. Annoyed and frustrated, he punched his fist through the big blue abstract canvas before shoving his hands into his hair.

He had to get out of his studio, get out of the warehouse. He couldn't think in here, couldn't create, couldn't paint. The portraits of Sage were all facing the wall but he knew that they were there and he was constantly tempted to turn them around, to waste minutes and hours looking at her glorious face, remembering how they loved each other.

Your choice, moron.

It had been two weeks since he'd seen her and he'd spent every minute of each day missing her. The news was out that Lachlyn was a Ballantyne and the press had gone nuts, as he'd expected. Surprisingly, Sage's pregnancy wasn't reported on and, for big mercies, he was grateful.

He'd called Lachlyn to find out if she was okay,

if she needed his help to deal with the press, but she'd moved into The Den and he heard that Linc had hired a bodyguard to accompany her wherever she went until the furor died down. The press had camped outside his warehouse for half a day but wet, snow-tinged rain had sent them scurrying back into their holes.

He had to get out of this place, get some fresh air. Tyce walked out of his studio and onto the catwalk and heard voices below him.

"You guys do know that this is breaking and entering, don't you? We could be arrested for this." Tyce immediately recognized Beckett's voice so he rested his forearms on the catwalk and waited to see what they were doing.

A voice he'd never heard before replied in a laconic drawl. "*I'll* be arrested and my PI license will be revoked since I picked the lock."

Linc walked further into the warehouse, followed by Jaeger and Beckett and lastly, a guy he didn't recognize. Unlike Sage's brothers, Mr. Ex-Military's eyes were darting around the warehouse looking for threats. His eyes shot upward and immediately clocked Tyce standing on the catwalk.

Super soldier—because the guy was a fighter, anyone could see that—gave him a quick nod.

"Whose stupid-ass idea was this anyway?" Jaeger muttered.

"Mine," Linc said, his voice rock hard. "I'm done with the situation and we're going to sort it out. I don't care if he has six black belts and a lightsaber, the imbecile is going to listen to us. If that takes one of us getting the crap kicked out of us, then so be it."

Tyce lifted his eyebrows at the desperation he heard in Linc's voice but he still remained quiet.

"Speak for yourself," Jaeger said.

"Reame can handle him," Beck said.

"You never told me that he had a couple of black belts," Reame said, looking amused. He looked up at Tyce. "Do you?"

Tyce almost smiled when three heads shot up to look at him. "A couple. In Tae Kwon Do and Krav Maga."

Reame swore and held up his hands. "He's all yours," he told the Ballantyne brothers, but Tyce knew whose side he'd be on if blows were traded. It wasn't his. As always, he was alone.

"What the hell do you want?" he demanded. "And what's so important that you broke into my place to tell me?"

"No breaking, only entering. I'm Reame Jepson, by the way."

He'd heard of Linc's oldest friend, the man the Ballantyne siblings had known since they were children. Not only were they great friends but the ex-soldier's company also handled the security for Ballantyne International and, from what he understood, many other Fortune 500 companies. Tyce gave Reame a brief nod but kept his eyes on Linc. "Say what you have to say, then get the hell out of my warehouse."

Linc nodded. "Okay. So this is what you need to know… Sage loves you."

She'd said that and maybe she believed it to be true but it wasn't enough. Love, sex, attraction wasn't enough. It was easier, better, safer to be on his own. "So?"

"We're here because my sister is miserable and looks like a corpse."

"Again, so? What do you want me to do?"

"I thought you said he was intelligent," Reame said to Jaeger, still sounding amused.

"I was wrong," Jaeger replied. "He's as dumb as a post."

Linc tossed him a curse and threw up his hands. "Can you all please concentrate?" He gripped the bridge of his nose with his fingers. Back in control, he looked up at Tyce again. "What I, we, want you to do is to tell her that you love her and then tell the world that you are thrilled to be the father of her child. I want to be able to tell the world that our family is expanding and we're excited that you and Lachlyn are part of our family. But really, I—we—just want Sage to be happy."

Tyce felt like he'd been hit by a piece of Canadian maple. He just stared at Linc, trying to assimilate his words. He knew that Linc was happy to have Lachlyn as part of the family but he never thought that Sage's brothers might feel the same about him.

Jaeger cleared his throat and Tyce's eyes bounced from his to Sage's second-eldest brother. "Did you ever consider that maybe your quest for Lachlyn to be part of a family was something you, subconsciously, needed? Maybe you were projecting your need for a family onto her."

"That's deep," Reame mocked, his mouth quirking.

"Shut up, half-wit," Jaeger muttered.

Tyce ignored their insults, thinking about Jaeger's comment. Was there any truth in his statement, any at all? Tyce gripped the banister as he considered his question and faced the obvious truth. Yes, he'd also wanted to be part of a family, wanted people he could lean on, people who would stand in his corner, who would fight for and with him.

He was used to walking alone, fighting his own battles. It was what he knew, what he felt comfortable doing and when Sage offered him something bigger, something he didn't know how to handle, he shot her down in flames. He thought he'd, one day, be okay with it. After all, he knew how to be an army of one.

He wasn't okay with it and walking away from her had frickin' ripped his heart and soul in two. Not to be melodramatic or anything.

"Do you know how much courage it took for Sage to open herself up to you, to ask for something more?" Linc demanded.

"She pushes people away!" Tyce protested, trying to grasp a straw that wasn't there.

"Sure, until she asked you to step in the ring with her. And you still haven't realized that when Sage pushes the hardest is when she most wants someone to push her back and not take no for an answer."

Jaeger sent him a cocky smile. "She might be our sister but she's a hell of a catch, Latimore. And you walked away from her? Moron."

Linc's fist slammed into Jaeger's biceps. "You are not helping!"

Tyce was barely aware of the hissed argument going on below him. He felt like Linc had handed him a new pair of glasses and a fuzzy world had just become clear. Linc's words resonated deep inside him and he knew them to be pure truth.

Sage had stepped way out of her comfort zone to ask him to love her and, God, he now, finally, could appreciate it. With this new knowledge, the last pieces of the puzzle that made up the full picture of his lover, his only love, fell into place.

She was his *it*, that indefinable, amazing, better part of his soul. He needed to go to her, to sort this out, but…

Hell. There was a damn good chance that he'd blown his opportunity with her, that she'd refuse to allow him back into her life. Tyce pushed his shoulders back, determination coursing through him. To hell with that. He did love her and Sage did need someone to push her back, to not take no for an answer. And he was the man to do it. He'd bucked the system all his life but, at the most important time, he'd walked away from the most vital thing in his life.

Jaeger, this one time, was right. Tyce was a moron.

He walked across the catwalk and jogged down

the stairs to the concrete floor below. He looked at Linc. "I hear you."

"Hearing is one thing but are you going to do something about it?"

Tyce nodded. "I am."

Beck cleared his throat and sent him a smile that shriveled his sack. "Good to know. Now, there's just one more thing we need to do."

"What's that?"

Jaeger cocked his head. "You made Sage cry," he said, sounding like he was ordering a cup of coffee.

Oh, crap. They said they'd rip him apart if he made Sage cry and judging by their hard expressions, she'd been crying a lot. Well, he was a fighter; he could tolerate three punches. Once it was done, they could all move on.

"Jesus," he muttered as he stood in front of the three Ballantyne brothers, bracing himself for what was to come. "Okay, take your hit."

Jaeger and Beck exchanged looks and Reame just grinned. Jaeger lifted a dark eyebrow, his eyes dark and cold. "You're going to make it right with Sage?"

Tyce nodded. "I already said that, didn't I? Yeah, I'm going to make it right." Damn, waiting for a punch was worse than the punch itself.

"If you hurt her again, we'll set Reame on you and he's a sneaky son of a bitch with mad skills. He'd do some damage," Beck told him, echoing Jaeger's icy demeanor.

"Understood." Tyce nodded. He looked at Linc, relieved that he'd avoided being hit by Sage's hot-headed brothers. They were more gracious than he might have been if some guy messed Lachlyn around. Linc looked like he always did, calm and controlled.

Okay then, dodged a bullet. Phew.

Tyce pulled in a breath, started to take his hands out of his pockets, thinking that he'd invite them upstairs. The big fist came out of nowhere, slammed into his jaw and he dropped backward, his butt connecting with the cold and very hard concrete. Crap, that hurt. Tyce looked up at Linc, who had a self-satisfied smile on his face.

Right, he hadn't seen that coming, Tyce thought, holding his jaw. "God, it hurts like a mother," he moaned.

"Good." Linc held out his hand to Tyce to pull him up. "You got coffee? We still have business to discuss before you go groveling back to Sage. And you will grovel."

"I will grovel," Tyce agreed, allowing Linc to pull him up. Holding his jaw, he lifted his eyebrows. "What business?"

Linc gestured to an amused Jaeger and Beck. "We're going to repay you the money you spent buying Lach-Ty shares. We inherited Connor's money so we'll spend it to reimburse you for Lachlyn's share of the company. We'll also add her as a co-owner of the assets we own jointly, like the art collection, the properties and the gem collection."

Holy crap, now he was really seeing stars. Tyce wiggled his jaw and started to lead them to the stairs.

As his foot hit the bottom stair, an idea popped into his head. "If I ask you to, do you think you could get Sage somewhere for me?"

"Possibly," Linc replied.

"And instead of reimbursing me for what I paid for the shares, could we do a swap?"

"What swap?" Jaeger asked, his eyes still amused. Yeah, it would be a while before he lived that punch down.

"There's a red diamond ring in your family collection that Sage loves. I'd rather have the stone than the money because I'd like to put it on your sister's finger."

Linc looked at him, then looked at his brothers. Some sort of silent communication happened between them and Linc finally nodded. "I think we can work that out."

Reame was the last one up the stairs and Tyce heard his chuckle. "I have to say that life is never boring with you Ballantynes."

Now there was a statement Tyce fully agreed with.

Thirteen

Sage didn't want to go to an art exhibition and she deeply resented her bossy future sisters-in-law— sadly, her brothers were rubbing off on them—turning up at her apartment and bundling her into the shower. Amy had always been bossy so that wasn't anything new. Art exhibition, cocktails and clubbing, they told her. Just the five of them setting Manhattan alight.

Ugh. The last thing in the world she felt like doing was having a girls' night out: the point of which was to drink copious amounts of alcohol to make you forget about your lousy man and to give you the courage to dance with, possibly kiss, some random guy. She was pregnant and the thought of kissing anyone else but Tyce made her want to throw up. What she most wanted to do was to go over to Tyce's warehouse to beg him, again, to reconsider her offer, to plead with him to love her.

Stupid heart, wanting what it couldn't have. So, not having an excuse to stay in—being pregnant and miserable wasn't a good enough excuse for the women in her life—she was out and about and wearing this silly dress with her bigger-than-normal boobs on display. It was a baby doll dress in a multicolored print and it effectively hid her blossoming baby bump.

"Take me home," Sage begged as they piled out of a taxi in front of the gallery where she and Tyce met again several months ago. She frowned at Piper. "Why are we here? They don't have an exhibition scheduled. And why are all the lights off?"

"It's an exhibition by a Norwegian installation artist, something to do with bioluminescence," Piper replied, tucking her hand into Sage's arm. "It's got to be dark to see the effect of the art."

"Don't want to go," Sage said, digging her heels in and looking at the cab. "I'm tired and my ankles are swollen and I have a backache."

Okay, she was whining but she couldn't do art, any type of art, right now. Was she asking too much to be allowed to nurse her weeping, bleeding heart in peace? Her mind was too full of Tyce as it was; memories of what they did and said to each other replayed on the megascreen of her mind, and coming back to this place, the place where they met, was simply too much for her.

She missed him so much she felt like she was walking around with a fraction of her heart.

"You're not far along enough to be complaining about a backache and swollen ankles," Cady told her, placing a hand in the middle of her back and pushing her toward the door.

"And you're not carrying twin boys so I have no sympathy for you," Piper added.

Tate rubbed Piper's big bump and smiled. "Fifteen minutes, Sage, and then we will take you wherever you want to go."

Sage perked up at that suggestion. "Home?"

"If that's what you want," Tate replied as they walked up the flight of stairs to the front door. Tate pulled the door open and ushered her into the dark gallery. Sage rolled her eyes at the complete darkness. Honestly some of these exhibitions were just ridiculous and in trying to do something weird and wonderful they forgot to be practical. How was she supposed to see the art if she couldn't see two inches in front of her face? Anyone could trip, she could bump into people...

Speaking of, why didn't she hear any chatter, why was the gallery so very silent?

Light flooded into the room and Sage blinked, her eyes needing a moment to refocus. Well, that was going to ruin the impact of the bioluminescence.

Sage immediately, instinctively, looked right to the spot where she first met Tyce and frowned at the massive blue abstract oil hanging on the wall. It held the outline of what looked like a woman's back and bottom and to the right of where her head should be; she could clearly see a fist-size hole in the canvas.

Sage gasped, recognizing the painting as being the one Tyce pushed her against when he made love to her that night in his studio. Barely breathing, she slowly looked around the gallery and when she saw what was on the walls, the room started to spin.

All his portraits were hanging on the walls, a good portion of which were of her. There were some of his mom, some of Lachlyn, many of random New Yorkers—from street people to buskers and servers— and they were all fantastic. Only the big blue abstract painting and the portraits of her, and of Lachlyn and his mom, had not-for-sale stickers on them.

Sage held her face, in awe of his talent. It was a small exhibition, roughly and quickly tossed together but it was that much more powerful for it. This wasn't slick and smooth, it was rough and tender and…open. This was Tyce allowing the world to look inside.

That type of vulnerability took courage and heart. So much heart. Pity that she had no claim on it.

Sage heard heavy footsteps behind her and slowly turned to watch Tyce walk across the room toward her, hands in the pockets of a pair of black dress slacks, his white dress shirt tucked in. God, he was so beautiful, Sage thought, in the most masculine way. Tough and tall, with his enigmatic eyes and strong face.

Sage's first instinct was to throw herself into his arms, to gush over his art, to demand to know why he was holding this portrait exhibition. Why now?

Why here, at this place from their past? Then she remembered that this was the man who'd tossed her love away, who'd rejected her heart. She didn't know why she was here—her sisters-in-law were in big, big trouble.

Overwhelmed, Sage turned around and headed toward the door, tears burning her eyes.

"Please don't cry. And please don't go," Tyce quietly said and she heard the longing and uncertainty in his voice. She stopped but kept her back to him, furiously brushing tears away with her fingertips.

Sage felt Tyce's big hands on her shoulders before his hands moved down her arms and encircled her waist, holding her against him. "Please don't go," he whispered, his mouth against her temple.

"Why should I stay?"

"You should stay—" Tyce's voice rumbled in her ear "—because I am the world's biggest idiot for letting you go, then and now. You should stay because you make my world brighter, my thinking clearer, my world turn. You should stay because we have a baby to raise and I'd like us to do that together."

Sage felt the first sparks of hope and ruthlessly smothered them. She pushed against his arm and he immediately released her. He looked tired, she thought, drawn, his face whiter than normal. His eyes glinted with uncertainty and worry and an emotion that went deeper than that, that might be, dare she think it, love?

"I'm sorry I wasn't brave, before." Tyce cradled her face in his hands and kissed her softly, his lips giving hers a quick caress. She wanted more and judging by his tense body, so did he but he drew back and lifted his mouth from hers. "I want us to stop hoping and dreaming and be more."

Sage stared at him, uncomprehending.

"I want you in my bed and in my life, being the first person I see every morning and the last person I see at night. I want that for the rest of my life. I want our kid, or kids, to fly into our bedroom and jump on the bed, on us. I want us, Sage. You and me. I need you."

God, she felt so humbled, so in awe of his courage to do this again, to open himself up to her again.

"I know that your instinct is to push me away, Sage, but I'm asking you not to. And I'm telling you that if you do, every time you do, I'm going to hold you tighter, love you more." Tyce pushed her hair off her forehead and rested his head on hers. "One more time, Sage, please. Be brave, for us. Take a chance on me."

"Tyce." Sage gripped his arms, feeling dizzy.

"Is that another no?" Tyce asked, worry in his eyes. No, not worry, soul-deep fear.

"No, it's not a no. I mean… God, yes. Please." Sage knew that she was messing up her words and cursed her thick tongue.

"You're going to have to be clearer than that, honey."

Yes, she realized that. Holding his arms for balance, she looked up into his exotic, sexy face, the one she'd missed so much. "I'll be brave—I'm not going to push you away, I promise."

"And you don't break your promises," Tyce murmured as a spark returned to his eyes.

"I promise to love you, whether we have six weeks or sixty years."

"I'm planning on sixty years," Tyce told her.

Sage lifted her arms and wound them around Tyce's neck.

Tyce kissed her temple, her cheek, the corner of her mouth as she murmured the words she so needed to say, that he needed to hear. "I love you. I miss you. I'm so, so sorry I hurt you."

Their kisses were softer, gentler, simply tasting their new beginning, testing out how love felt in sunlight instead of shadows. Passion rumbled but they both pushed it away; passion was for later. This was something new, something that needed a little attention, a bit of nurturing.

Five, ten or twenty minutes could have passed when Tyce pulled his mouth and hands off her but was keeping her plastered against his long frame. Sage rested her cheek against his chest and nodded. This was where she belonged.

Tyce's hand stroked her hair. "We still need to talk, sweetheart."

Sage wrinkled her nose. "Do we have to? I'm kind of liking this."

Tyce smiled, pure sunshine in his eyes. Yeah, those shadows were gone and it was about time.

"I am too but we have a bunch of people in the back room and they are getting anxious."

"What? Who? Carol and her assistants?" Sage asked, thinking of the gallery owner and her staff. She gestured to his art. "And is this a real exhibition? Are you going to sell your portraits?"

Tyce looked around. "Yeah, I think so. Should I keep it low-key like this or give it to a high-end gallery?"

"I like this," Sage replied, walking into the middle of the room but keeping her hand in his. "I think the portraits need a smaller, more intimate space. I think you should keep it as it is but—" she pointed to the ruined abstract in that prominent position "—that goes." She sent him an amused look. "I thought we had an agreement about you not exhibiting anything that had any connection to our love life."

Tyce wrapped his arm around her waist. "It stays. It makes me laugh."

"It's awful, Tyce," Sage protested.

"Yeah, but everyone will wonder why it's there and will concoct all sorts of crazy ideas about it and only you and I will know the truth."

For him to leave that awful painting hanging on the wall was his way of telling her, and the world, that he was finally secure about his talent as an artist, his place in the world. "But why does it have a hole in it?" Sage asked.

"I was standing in front of it, thinking about you, and I was so pissed off that I punched it."

"Talking about punches, why do you have a bruise on your jaw?" Sage asked, her eyes narrowing.

"Oh, that's courtesy of your brother," Tyce replied, his tone blasé.

"Jaeger punched you?" Sage shrieked.

"Linc, and it happened five minutes before he told me that you Ballantynes are repaying me for Lachlyn's shares. Was that your idea?"

Sage wrinkled her nose. "If Connor had known about Lachlyn then that's what would have happened. The money should be with you in a month or two—did Linc explain that?"

Tyce's hand caressed her back. "Some of the money will be in my back account. Not much but more than I had before."

Sage stepped away from him and put her hands on her hips. "What do you mean by that? I know that we all signed papers to transfer our share of the assets, to liquidate the cash."

Tyce's hands slid into the pockets of his pants. "Yep, but I'm diverting some of that money back into the Ballantyne coffers. Well, Linc and I are still arguing about this. He says that the object in question belongs to you, that it's right for you to own it, but I'd still like to pay for it."

Object? What object? What on earth was he talking about? Tyce opened his hand and Sage looked at a small square of white tissue paper resting in his palm.

"Trying to buy a ring for a jewelry designer is a bitch so I thought that I'd try something else."

"A ring?" Sage asked, knowing that she sounded stupid but not quite believing what she was hearing.

Tyce flipped open the tissue paper to reveal the brilliance of the red diamond flower ring. "Like this stone, you are rare and precious and you take my breath away. Will you please, please marry me?"

Sage stared at the ring, tears burning her eyes. "My mom's ring. Oh my God, Tyce, that's my mom's red diamond!" Sage reached out to pick up the ring but Tyce snapped his fist closed. Sage jerked her head up and saw the mischief in his eyes.

"You Ballantynes… You see gemstones and everything instantly goes out your head." Tyce waved his closed fist in front of her face. "Say yes and you can have the ring."

"Are you bribing me?" Sage demanded, smiling, her hand holding his fist.

"Apparently so," Tyce said. "So, are you going to marry me for your mom's ring?"

Sage reached up to hold his face. "I am going to marry you because I am stupidly in love with you and I intend to stay that way for the rest of my life. Because I can't imagine myself being with anyone else but you." She smiled, teasing him. "But I can't lie, the ring is a factor."

Tyce kissed her, his lips curving against her mouth. "I'll take it. Love you, babe."

"And it's about damn time!"

Sage whipped around to see her brothers, their wives, Amy, Reame and Lachlyn walking from the storeroom at the back, the men carrying bottles of champagne and the women carrying glasses.

After kissing Lachlyn—she had another sister, yay!—Sage narrowed her eyes and looked at Tyce. "Why are they here?"

"I needed their help to set this all up, to get you here," Tyce said, shrugging. "Apparently they have their uses."

Sage heard the affection under his sarcasm and thought that he and her brothers would be just fine. She, however, was not. Sage walked up to Linc and poked her finger in his chest. "What the hell were you thinking, punching Tyce? Seriously, what is wrong with you?"

Linc brushed her hand away. "He deserved it." Linc kissed her cheek and gave her a quick hug. Sage hugged him back and felt him stiffen in her arms. She pulled away and found him looking at the destroyed canvas. "What the hell is that?" he demanded.

Jaeger also tipped his head to the side and sent Tyce a look of pure confusion. "I don't get it, Latimore. They pay you for this garbage?"

Tyce and Sage exchanged a long look filled with everything they were going to spend the rest of their lives saying. *I love you. You're gorgeous. Can't wait to get you naked.*

Tyce laughed and shrugged. "Yep. Strange but true."

"What's it called?" Jaeger asked, moving closer to the wall.

Sage's eyes didn't waver from Tyce's face. "It's called *Love, Lost and Found.*"

Tyce's eyes warmed and softened at her answer and he wore his love and devotion for her like a coat of armor. She'd finally found her warrior and damn, it felt amazing.

"You Ballantynes are so weird," Reame said, popping the cork on a bottle of champagne. He looked at Lachlyn and raised his brows. "Their madness is contagious. Run… Run now."

Tyce grinned at Reame. "It's not madness—it's love." He looked from Reame to Lachlyn and smiled. "You two should try it—it's not so bad."

Reame and Lachlyn looked equally horrified and Sage smiled at their expression. Actually, come to think of it, her new sister and the man Sage considered her fourth brother looked really good together…

* * * * *

If you liked Sage's story,
pick up these other
BALLANTYNE BILLIONAIRES *books from*
Joss Wood!

HIS EX'S WELL-KEPT SECRET
REUNITED...AND PREGNANT
THE CEO'S NANNY AFFAIR

as well as reader favorite
MARRIED TO THE MAVERICK MILLIONAIRE

Available now from Harlequin Desire!

***

If you're on Twitter, tell us what you think of
Harlequin Desire! #harlequindesire

Get 2 Free Books,
Plus 2 Free Gifts—
just for trying the Reader Service!

*Billionaire Broderick Steele was raised to hate his rival,
Glenna Mikkelson-Powers—even if she's the sexiest woman he's
ever known. Then, amid corporate mergers and scandal, they
find an abandoned baby who could be Broderick's...or Glenna's.
Playing house has never been so high stakes!*

Read on for a sneak peek of
THE BABY CLAIM
by USA TODAY bestselling author Catherine Mann,
*the first book in the **ALASKAN OIL BARONS** saga!*

Being so close to this man had never been a wise idea.

The sensual draw was too strong for any woman to resist for
long and stay sane. Broderick's long wool duster over his suit was
pure Hugo Boss. But the cowboy hat and leather boots had a hint of
wear that only increased his appeal. His dark hair, which attested to
his quarter-Inuit heritage, showed the first signs of premature gray.
His charisma and strength were as vast as the Alaskan tundra they
both called home.

In a state this large, there should have been enough space for
both of them. Theoretically, they should never have to cross paths.
But their feuding families' constant battle over dominance of the
oil industry kept Glenna Mikkelson-Powers and Broderick Steele
in each other's social circles.

Too often for her peace of mind.

Even so, he'd never shown up at her office before.

Light caught the mischief in his eyes, bringing out whiskey
tones in the dark depths. His full lips pulled upward in a haughty
smile.

"You're being highly unprofessional." She narrowed her own
eyes, angry at her reaction to him as she drank in his familiar
arrogance.

Their gazes held and the air crackled. She remembered the feeling all too well from their *Romeo and Juliet* fling in college.

Doomed from the start.

He was her rival. His mesmerizing eyes and broody disposition would not distract her.

She jabbed a manicured finger in his direction. "Your father is up to something."

She scooped up a brass paperweight in the shape of a bear that had belonged to her father. Shifting it from hand to hand was an oddly comforting ritual. Or perhaps not so odd. When she was a small girl, her father had told her the statue gave people power, attributing his success to the brass bear. After the last year of loss, Glenna needed every ounce of luck and power she could get.

"There's no need to threaten me with your version of brass knuckles." Humor left his face and his expression became all business. "But since you're as bemused by what's happening as I am, come with me to speak to your mother."

"Of course. Let's do that. We'll have this sorted out in no time."

The sooner the better.

She wanted Broderick Steele out of her office and not a simple touch away.

Want to give in to temptation with
steamy tales of irresistible desire?

Check out **Harlequin® Presents®,
Harlequin® Desire** and
Harlequin® Kimani™ Romance books!

New books available every month!

CONNECT WITH US AT:

Harlequin.com/Community

 Facebook.com/HarlequinBooks

 Twitter.com/HarlequinBooks

 Instagram.com/HarlequinBooks

 Pinterest.com/HarlequinBooks

ReaderService.com

**ROMANCE WHEN
YOU NEED IT**

PGENRE2017

LOVE
Harlequin
romance?

Join our Harlequin community to share your thoughts and connect with other romance readers!

Be the first to find out about promotions, news, and exclusive content!

Sign up for the Harlequin e-newsletter and download a free book from any series at

www.TryHarlequin.com

THE WORLD IS BETTER WITH

Romance

Harlequin has everything from contemporary, passionate and heartwarming to suspenseful and inspirational stories.

Whatever your mood, we have a romance just for you!

Connect with us to find your next great read, special offers and more.

f /HarlequinBooks

🐦 @HarlequinBooks

www.HarlequinBlog.com

www.Harlequin.com/Newsletters

H HARLEQUIN®

A *Romance* FOR EVERY MOOD™

www.Harlequin.com

Reward the book lover in you!

Earn points from all your Harlequin book purchases from wherever you shop.

Turn your points into *FREE BOOKS* of your choice
OR
EXCLUSIVE GIFTS from your favorite authors or series.

Join for FREE today at
www.HarlequinMyRewards.com.

Harlequin My Rewards is a free program (no fees) without any commitments or obligations.